nickelodeon

THE JUNIOR NOVELIZATION

© 2023 Paramount Pictures. All Rights Reserved.
Nickelodeon, Teenage Mutant Ninja Turtles, and all related titles, logos, and characters are trademarks of Viacom International Inc.
Based on characters created by Peter Laird and Kevin Eastman.
Published in the United States by Random House Children's Books, a division of Penguin Random House LLC, 1745 Broadway, New York, NY 10019, and in Canada by Penguin Random House Canada Limited, Toronto.
Random House and the colophon are registered trademarks of Penguin Random House LLC.
rhcbooks.com
ISBN 978-0-593-64711-0 (trade)
Printed in the United States of America
10 9 8 7 6 5 4 3 2 1

nickelodeon

THE JUNIOR NOVELIZATION

Based on the screenplay by
Seth Rogen & **Evan Goldberg** & **Jeff Rowe,**
and **Dan Hernandez** & **Benji Samit**

Adapted by **David Lewman**

RANDOM HOUSE NEW YORK

TIME!
12:40 science!
NO RATS ALLOWED!
RAPH
HOME
WEAPON ROOM
TOILET
OUT
KITCHEN
TECH ROOM
DIOACTIVE MATTER
WASTE
THE STEELY BOYS
TURTLE POWER!
RAPH
UH OH
GO RHINOS
APRIL
SWORD 2
TO SEWER

Late one night, an armored van tore through the streets of New York City. Inside, soldiers for the T.C.R.I. (the Techno-Cosmic Research Institute) listened to instructions from their leader, a tall, muscular man whose nickname was Spider. Just by looking at his gruff face, anyone could tell that Spider expected instant obedience from his troops. And got it. Or else.

"Listen up!" Spider barked. "I'm gonna make this simple. We're going after Dr. Baxter Stockman, the former head of T.C.R.I.'s Mutant Development wing. He stole billions of dollars' worth of research, including an actual mutant specimen!"

The soldiers exchanged nervous glances. This was

the first they'd heard about going after a mutant. What might this mutant be capable of?

"Each of you has been issued a high-powered anti-mutant weapon," Spider continued, holding up a blaster. "Whatever Stockman's made, this can unmake it!"

Spider scanned the soldiers' faces, hoping this information would give them confidence. But they still looked anxious. Some of them were even sweating, though it wasn't a hot night. Spider needed them pumped up and ready for action. He opened a laptop with a video feed, figuring a pep talk from the boss might help. "Okay. From headquarters, the head of T.C.R.I. herself, Dr. Cynthia Utrom, has a few words."

Dr. Utrom appeared on the screen, looking cold and menacing. "This mission is of the utmost importance," she snarled. "Failure will be . . . frowned upon. Bring Stockman's mutant and whatever he used to make it."

The soldiers exchanged glances. So not only was there a mutant, but they were supposed to bring it in? What kind of wild mission was this, anyway?

Drip . . . drip . . . drip . . .

In the basement of an abandoned building, exposed pipes dripped rusty water into foul puddles. Ignoring his shabby surroundings, Dr. Baxter Stockman mixed chemicals into a vial of green ooze. "I've done it, little one!" the proud genius cried triumphantly. "I've perfected the ooze! Are you excited for Daddy?"

He looked down toward the floor. There, in an old playpen, sat a human baby with the head, wings, and limbs of a fly. Buzzing happily, it ate sugar from a large sack. Stockman took off his white lab coat and bent down to lovingly wrap it around the fly-baby.

"Not too much sugar!" He chuckled. "You'll spoil your dinner." He patted the fly-baby on the back affectionately. "You know," he mused, "my so-called *friends* at T.C.R.I. want to use you as a weapon." Stockman shook his head. "I couldn't allow that." He stood up straight and looked around the gloomy chamber. "But we're safe now. And soon you'll have brothers and sisters!"

The scientist crossed to a shelf holding green vials full of cells. Above each vial was a drawing of a mutant:

A humanoid warthog. A lizard man. An crocodile with long arms.

"See?" Stockman said, gesturing toward the vials. "They're already growing. A real family for both of us. I never had a family, little one. No friends. Nobody ever liked me. Or even accepted me. But now I think we can be happy." He picked up a set of blueprints for a large, complicated device and studied the diagrams. "Very, very happy . . ."

BANG!

Stockman looked up, startled and frightened by the loud noise echoing through the empty floor upstairs. Someone was trying to break in!

Outside, Spider urged his fellow warriors to keep slamming a battering ram into the derelict building's locked door. "Again!" he ordered.

WHAM! With a powerful blow, the soldiers cracked the door open. "Go, go, go!" Spider shouted. The armed soldiers ran into the dark building. They headed down the basement stairs, soon finding their way into Stockman's secret laboratory.

The scientist was frantically trying to pack up his

research equipment. He held a glass vial of green ooze.

"Freeze! Don't move!" Spider yelled, pointing his weapon right at Stockman. "Where is the specimen?" he asked, referring to the mutant taken from T.C.R.I.'s facility.

"I—I . . . uh . . . ," Stockman stammered, trying to stall for time, desperate to save his creation. His child. His family.

The team of soldiers found the empty playpen. "It's not here," said Spider. Then, worried that Stockman would somehow command the mutant to attack, Spider added, "Stay quiet."

But the fly-baby didn't need to be commanded.

"YAAAAHHH!" a soldier screamed as the creature flew right at him, knocking him to the floor. One by one, the soldiers were taken out by the rampaging fly-baby. A soldier waved his weapon wildly, trying to get the buzzing mutant in his sights.

"Don't shoot!" Spider ordered. "We need it alive!" He turned his attention from the furious insect-child to tell Stockman, "Don't move."

Seizing its opportunity, the fly-baby attacked

Spider. Screaming, he fired his weapon, disobeying his own order.

"No!" Stockman shouted. "Don't shoot! The chemicals in this room are highly explosive!"

But his warning came too late. Spider fired his weapon again—

BOOM!

Chemicals flashed and burst into flames.

"No!" Stockman cried, leaping toward the fly-baby to shield it with his body. The full force of the chemical blast whooshed across the room, enveloping him and the fly-baby. When the smoke cleared, Stockman was still lying on the floor, gripping the vial of green ooze in his blistered hand.

The fly-baby was nowhere to be seen.

Dusting himself off, Spider scanned the room. The floor was littered with the unconscious bodies of Stockman and Spider's fellow soldiers. A call came in from the head of T.C.R.I. to check on the team's progress.

"Cynthia, I'm sorry," Spider told Utrom. "We lost everything."

At T.C.R.I. headquarters, Cynthia Utrom sat in a huge room, surrounded by looming pieces of complex machinery and bubbling vats of chemicals. A group of scientists looked at her expectantly, eager to hear the results of the soldiers' mission.

"Bring me anything else you find," Utrom ordered. "We'll copy his research, no matter how long it takes. Baxter Stockman's creation must live on! And with it a new form of life itself!" Cynthia laughed maniacally. Her scientists looked at each other uneasily.

Back in Stockman's lab, the soldiers gathered up the few remnants that hadn't been destroyed by the fire. They also lifted Stockman himself. As the life drained from his body, he dropped the vial of green ooze. The soldiers didn't notice.

The vial rolled toward a sewer grate and fell into the inky abyss, setting in motion a chain of events no one—not even the brilliant Baxter Stockman himself—could have ever anticipated.

Fifteen years later, in the sewers under New York City, four Teenage Mutant Ninja Turtles grabbed their ninja weapons—swords, sai, nunchucks, bo staff—and set out on a night raid. Running in formation, they sprinted through a sewer pipe that opened near the Brooklyn Bridge and leapt into action!

Moments later, in a dark alley, Leonardo, the leader of the four brothers, pulled out an ancient-looking scroll. "Master Splinter has given us a very important mission tonight," he said in a low, raspy voice. "We must use stealth and cunning to infiltrate the human world and retrieve . . . yogurt!"

Making fun of his brother's voice, Donatello echoed,

"Yogurt! We need to infiltrate the world to get yogurt!"

"Yogurt!" Raphael said, also mocking Leo's voice. "I'm trying to be cool, so I'm talking in a deep voice."

"Okay, Batman," Michelangelo added sarcastically. "Don't hurt your throat!"

Leo looked annoyed. "I'm just trying to hype you guys up!"

Raphael grabbed the scroll out of his brother's hands. "Gimme that list. What else are we getting?" He read the shopping—or more accurately, the *stealing*—list out loud: "Four quarts of nonfat milk, ice cream, fruits and veggies—"

"Gross," Michelangelo interrupted, making a face.

"—and a party-sized bag of ranch-dressing-flavored chips," Raphael concluded.

"I like cheese puffs," Michelangelo put in, hoping this might be added to their list of items. His brothers ignored him. They were well aware of Mikey's love of cheese puffs. Tonight's task was to gather the items requested by their father, not their brother.

Donnie peered at the list. "Dad was very specific about wanting the party-sized bag. He underlined it twice!"

"All right," Leo said, putting the list away. "Donnie, you're on toiletries."

"Great," Donnie said unenthusiastically.

"Raph," Leo continued, "you're stocking up the pantry."

"Yeah, yeah, yeah." Raph sighed.

"And, Mikey, you're on junk food," Leo ordered.

"I'm thirsty," Mikey said. His brothers ignored this. Mikey was pretty much *always* hungry or thirsty.

"And remember," Leo concluded, "don't let any human see you! Because why?"

In unison, the four brothers recited, *"Humans are the demon scum of the earth. Don't say hi. They lust to murder that which is different from them. To interact with them is to die."*

"And Dad wouldn't have taught us that catchy rhyme if it wasn't true!" Leo said.

Mikey looked doubtful. "To be honest, I think humans are kinda cool. Beyoncé . . ."

"Drake!" Raph suggested.

"We wouldn't have K-pop without humans," Donnie pointed out. He was a big fan of Korean pop music, even though the radio and internet reception in the sewers wasn't great.

Leo nodded. "Sure. We all think humans are cool. But we've got a job to do." He lowered his voice again, speaking huskily. "Let's go."

Raph, Mikey, and Donnie again mocked Leo's deep delivery as they ran out of the alley into the night, intent on hunting down their prey: delicious groceries.

In a small bodega, which is a neighborhood store selling everything from umbrellas to vegetables, Leo stealthily covered the lens of a security camera. As the owner of the bodega watched an old sitcom on a small television, Raph rappelled down from the ceiling and used his sai blades to snatch a loaf of bread. As the Turtles silently crept away, Leo scratched *bread* off the list.

Sneaking across the docks at the edge of the East River, Mikey grabbed a toilet plunger from a shipping crate and tossed it to Leo.

On top of a high-rise apartment building, Raph and Donnie snipped fruits and veggies off the branches and vines of a rooftop garden.

Behind a fancy hotel, Donnie used his bo staff to

snag rolls of toilet paper from a delivery van.

Meanwhile, Leo and Mikey leapt onto the top of a moving truck. As it sped through the streets of lower Manhattan, they managed to swing down, pull up the back door, and tumble inside. When they saw the truck's delicious contents, the two brothers smiled. It was carrying bags of ranch-dressing-flavored chips—party-sized!

With every item crossed off their list, the brothers headed to their rendezvous point on top of a building in Midtown. Strictly speaking, it wasn't *necessary* for them to meet on the rooftop before heading home, but it made their shopping excursion seem more like a ninja adventure. As they climbed up separately, a news report played on a giant screen attached to the side of the building.

"Another brazen and deadly robbery today in the heart of Manhattan," a news anchor reported. "An industrial-grade generator, capable of powering all of Staten Island, was stolen mid-transport. Police fear that the incident is connected to recent thefts of plutonium, high-density conducting cables, and a nuclear power converter." File photos of each stolen item appeared on the screen as the anchor named them. "All the police have to go on at this point," he concluded, "is vague rumors of a mysterious criminal mastermind known on the streets as Superfly."

"Not bad!" Leo exclaimed as he vaulted over the low wall and landed on the roof, meeting his three brothers. "Heading home on a good note. Let's get these groceries back—"

"Whoa! Whoa!" Raph interrupted, holding up both hands. "We've only been out for an hour! Let's stay out!"

Donnie and Mikey clearly agreed with Raph's proposal. "Yeah!" Mikey urged Leo. "Come on!"

Leo couldn't believe what he was hearing. "Guys, come on! We said we weren't gonna do this anymore! Last week it was Madison Square Garden to watch the Knicks. The week before that it was an outdoor concert."

Mikey grinned, remembering the concert. "She hit them notes like crazy!"

"She was transcendent!" Raph said.

"My spirit left my body!" Donnie claimed.

Leo just shook his head. "If we keep taking so long to run a few quick errands, Splinter's gonna catch on. He'll ground us."

Shrugging this off, Donnie said, "He never goes anywhere, so he has no idea how long things take. For all he knows, it takes three hours to get to the bodega."

"We told him we wouldn't mess around anymore!" Leo argued.

But Donnie wasn't listening. He was busy checking his phone to see what might be going on around town that night. "Oh, hey!" he said, excited. "It's outdoor movie night in Dumbo!" Standing for "Down Under the Manhattan Bridge Overpass," Dumbo was a trendy neighborhood in Brooklyn.

"Nice!" Raph said, grinning.

"I hope it's an action movie," Donnie said.

"I hope it's a funny one!" Mikey said.

"Come on, come on," Donnie said, hurrying toward

the edge of the rooftop. "Let's go! Let's go! Let's go!" He, Raph, and Mikey started climbing down a fire escape.

Seeing that he was hopelessly outnumbered, Leo reluctantly followed his brothers. "Fine!" he called after them. "Wait up!"

The movie showing on the outdoor screen was *Ferris Bueller's Day Off*, a movie from the '80s about a high school dude who played hooky with his friends to enjoy one incredible day in Chicago. The four mutant Turtles watched from a nearby rooftop, entranced by the film.

"I wish I had hair like that," Mikey said wistfully.

"Look at that vest, man," Donnie said, pointing at the screen. "Dude, everyone is groovin' right now."

Leo was fascinated. "Is this how high school is in, like, real life?" He watched as Ferris danced on a float to the Beatles' "Twist and Shout."

Nodding, Raph said, "Yeah, if you go to high school, you can just hijack a parade whenever you want!"

"Wow," Mikey said, awed. "Can you imagine that?"

"Yeah, I'm totally not jealous at all," Donnie remarked,

saying the exact opposite of how he really felt.

The brothers' eyes wandered from the screen to the crowd of teenagers watching the movie and hanging out together. A guy put his arm around a girl. Some jocks tossed a football back and forth. A kid started dancing like the characters on the screen, and other kids threw popcorn at him, laughing.

Mikey started dancing, too, mimicking the actors on the screen. Leo pulled him out of sight. "Sit down."

Raph sighed. "Maybe one day we'll be able to dance in the streets and have crowds of people cheering for us, you know?"

"Yeah, yeah, maybe one day," Leo said sadly, not believing it for a second. He was pretty sure they were going to have to spend their lives alone, never making any friends outside their little family. He cleared a lump out of his throat. "Guys, let's go."

The brothers took a last look at all the teenagers enjoying themselves and at the movie screen. Then they turned and lowered themselves into the sewer. Mikey lingered a moment, looking through the grate at the shining lights of the city.

When they reached their home deep beneath the streets, the Turtles tried to sneak into their room unseen by their dad. "Everybody be quiet," Leo whispered. "Maybe he already went to sleep."

"Wait, why are we whispering?" Donnie asked.

"Whispering is like white noise," Mikey explained. "Good to sleep by." He started making a sound like static from a radio.

"Dude!" Leo hissed. "Too loud!"

CLICK!

A lamp snapped on. The four brothers were startled. *"AHHHH!"*

Their dad, a mutant rat named Splinter, was waiting for them. "Boys! Where have you been? I've been FREAKING OUT!"

The teens all tried to answer at once.

"We're sorry, Dad," Leo apologized.

"There was this cat," Mikey fibbed, "and you know I'm scared of cats . . ."

They tried to slink off to bed, but Splinter stopped them. "Wait! You said you would go shopping and come right back! Where were you?"

The brothers tried to come up with some excuse for their tardiness, but Splinter just stared at them, unconvinced. Finally, Leo said, "Look, we're really sorry, Dad. Some of the guys wanted to see a movie, and I tried to talk them out of it."

"LEO!" Raph, Donnie, and Mikey blurted out at the same time. They couldn't believe Leo was throwing them under the bus.

Splinter looked horrified. "You watched a movie? With HUMANS?!"

Mikey got in Leo's face. "You ratted us out!"

"Hey!" Splinter said, offended. "Don't use that word that way!"

"Sorry, Dad," Mikey said, looking sheepish.

Donnie tried to calm their father down. "It wasn't that big of a deal! We just watched a movie and came back. We're fine!"

Splinter frowned. "You forgot, huh? You don't remember why humans are disgusting monsters? Why they're dangerous? Why they're gonna milk us for our blood?!"

Donnie rolled his eyes. "Again with the milking . . ."

"They don't want to milk us, Dad," Mikey said.

"You know what?" Splinter said, staring at them. "I'm gonna tell the story again."

"No!" Leo groaned.

"Dad, we *hate* the story!" Mikey whined.

"It's such a bummer!" Donnie added.

"I'd rather have my teeth ripped out!" Raph complained.

Looking stern, Splinter folded his arms across his chest. "Just for that, I'll tell you the *long* version."

Defeated, the four brothers flopped down to endure the tale they'd heard their father tell many, many times before. As he recounted his story, Splinter acted it out, describing everything so vividly that the Turtles could easily picture the action.

"It all started fifteen years ago," Splinter began. "I was just a scrawny young rat, scavenging food off the streets of New York. I was at the bottom of the world! It was terrible! Nobody liked me. I had no friends. Raccoons did not like me. Dogs did not like me. You know who hated me the most? Humans! I had one friend. A cockroach. We got along very well. His name was Kevin. But a human stepped on him, so I ate him."

The Turtles made disgusted faces. This sickening detail really wasn't important to Splinter's story, but for some reason he always included it.

"One day, down in the sewers, everything changed," he continued. "I found four baby turtles covered in green ooze. You four!"

Mikey propped his chin on his fists. "Were we cute? I bet we were super cute!"

Splinter shrugged. "You were the first things I met that didn't want to kill me or eat me. One of you even nuzzled up against me."

"Which one?" Donnie asked. "Was it me?"

"Doubtful," Mikey said. "You're not really a nuzzler. I bet it was me."

Splinter raised his hands. "Who knows? Back then, you all look just alike to me. But I could not leave you. You were covered in this ooze that someone had dumped in the sewers. Whatever this stuff was, it transformed us. We turned into mutants!"

"Yeah, we know," Leo said impatiently. "You've told us all this before—"

"Quiet!" Splinter barked angrily. In a softer voice, he resumed his tale. "Because I was older, I became an older rat man. You guys were babies, so you stayed baby turtle boys. If you think about that, it couldn't make more sense."

He described running through the sewers with the baby Turtles. "It was weird, but we became a family. . . ." Getting a happy look on his face, the old rat described how the young Turtles danced to a record. Ate pizza together. Drew on the walls of the sewer. Crawled into bed with Splinter and slept with him. Enjoyed life below the streets together.

Until one day when the young Turtles saw the bright lights of the city through a sewer grate, so Splinter led them up into Times Square, one of the busiest parts of New York City. Colorful signs and screens lit the sides of tall buildings. Crowds of tourists and native New Yorkers hurried along the sidewalks and across the streets.

"As happy as we were," Splinter narrated, "you were always obsessed with the human world. So one day I thought maybe we should give it a shot. What was the worst that could happen?"

At first, in all the activity, no one noticed the human-sized rat and his four young wards. But then, a woman bumped into Splinter and said, "Oh, sorry. Excuse me . . ." She looked at him and screamed. "It's a rat man!"

"A rat man?!" a guy said.

"Everybody, look at the rat man!" someone else cried, pointing at Splinter.

A businessman looked skeptical. "It's just a person in a suit." But when he touched Splinter, he shouted, "No, it's real! A REAL RAT MAN!"

All the people on the sidewalk around Splinter and

the Turtles cried out at once. "Circle the rat!" "Chase the rat!" "Giant mutant rat!" "What're you doing here, RAT MAN?!" The terrified citizens and visitors started throwing bottles and trash at the mutant rat. Dodging this assault, Splinter lost his grip on the Turtles and watched, horrified, as they scattered in four separate directions.

"No! Boys!" he cried.

Scampering after the little Turtles, the old rat managed to scoop them up one by one until only Mikey was still missing. He spotted him heading toward a busy intersection. Slipping past shocked humans like a wide receiver, Splinter charged through the crowd and grabbed Mikey just before he was flattened by a speeding truck.

Splinter cradled the four Turtles in his arms. They smiled up at him, unaware of any danger.

"Surround him!" people screamed. "Don't let the rat man get away!"

Splinter dove into an open manhole, escaping from the humans with his precious cargo of four little mutant Turtles. "I promised to never let anyone hurt you again," he told the teens, coming to the end of his story. "I needed to find a way to unlock the ancient secrets of ninjutsu. How to turn a body into a weapon of death! And . . . I found it."

On the internet, Splinter watched martial arts training videos and passed the knowledge he gained on to his adopted sons. Practicing for years as they grew bigger and stronger, the four brothers became highly skilled . . . at least in theory, since Splinter never let them try out their skills against actual opponents.

"We thought we needed the human world," Splinter concluded, "but we only need each other. That is why I'm so strict! You boys are all I got. And you are all I'll ever have!"

Mikey shook his head. "You don't know that."

"Yes, I do!" Splinter insisted. "You know how hard it is to find other mutants my age? It's a really small pool. There's none! Zero! Zilch! We are *alone*!"

The Turtles looked away. They didn't like the idea of being alone for the rest of their lives. Would they really never meet anyone else, ever?

Splinter paced. "Look," he said, "I really don't want to do this, but no leaving the sewer for one month."

The Turtles jumped to their feet, shocked to be grounded for a whole month. "Seriously?!" Mikey squeaked.

"What?" Donnie yelped.

Splinter raised his hands and patted the air, trying to calm them down. "Yeah, I've made up my mind. That's it. I'm done."

Furious, Raph stormed out of the room. "This sucks!"

"Raph, come on," Leo said, trying to stop him. But Raph pushed him off and continued right on into their bedroom. Donnie and Mikey sadly followed Raph.

"Mikey?" Leo said, afraid his brothers weren't speaking to him.

"Was it worth it, Mr. Leader?" Donnie asked him sarcastically.

"Sorry!" Leo said. "I just . . . I can't lie to Dad." He trudged after the other three, following them into the bedroom, where they sat together discussing their awful fate.

Idly spinning his nunchucks, Mikey said, "Hey, guys, if we weren't monsters that were shunned by society and locked in a sewer by our crazy rat dad and could actually do what we wanted, what would you guys do?"

Donnie polished his bo staff with a cloth. "I mean, if I'm being honest, I'd just be normal. You know?"

Nodding, Raph said, "Yeah. Like go to high school."

"Yeah, be accepted," Donnie said.

"Yeah, that sounds dope," Mikey agreed.

Raph stood up and wandered the room. "I just gotta get out of this sewer, man! I like you guys and all, but I simply cannot live a happy life knowing that your faces are the last things I'm gonna see before I die!"

"Even if it's like this?" Donnie said, making a goofy face.

"No," Raph said. "But I like that face better than your normal face."

"Guess what," Leo said. "Living a normal life and going to high school? It's never gonna happen. So let's just stop talking about it."

The next night, two criminals walked down the street dressed as construction workers. They wore earpieces that allowed them to communicate. Their accomplice sat parked in an ice cream truck. "All right, focus up," he broadcast. "The truck containing the radioactive storage unit is one minute out."

"Copy that," one construction worker answered.

The truck driver said, "Let's not mess this up."

"Superfly does *not* take kindly to errors."

"Any of you met him?" the other construction worker asked.

"Nope," said the driver. "I hear he only meets through video conferences, and he never has his camera on."

"Any idea what he's building with all this weird equipment?" the first construction worker asked.

"Who cares?" his partner sneered. "Hey, as long as the check clears. Am I right?"

"Hey, hey, chill!" the truck driver hissed. "Target is approaching."

An armored truck with *T.C.R.I.* on the side sped down the street. The two guys dressed as construction workers tossed a long belt studded with sharp spikes across the road. *BAP! BAP! BAP! BAP!* The truck's tires were all punctured. With four flat tires, the truck's driver lost control and crashed into the side of a brick building. *KROOOOSH!*

"Sixty seconds till police response," the ice cream truck driver said. He quickly backed up his truck behind the disabled truck. The two construction guys attached explosives to the hinges of the truck's rear door and blew it open. *BOOM!* A mechanism extended from the back of the ice cream truck and swiftly transferred a large device from the T.C.R.I. truck to the ice cream truck.

"Thirty seconds," the driver said. "We gotta move!" The two guys disguised as construction workers piled into the ice cream truck, and the driver hit the gas. *VROOOM!* The ice cream truck peeled out with its stolen cargo. All in a matter of seconds!

Inside the ice cream truck, the criminals celebrated their successful theft. "Nice!" the first guy dressed as a construction worker whooped, high-fiving his partner.

"We crushed that mission!" the other construction guy crowed.

But then they heard sirens. *URRRRREEEE! WHOP! WHOP! WHOP!* A police car was right behind them with its lights flashing!

"I got this!" the driver of the ice cream truck shouted. "Hang on!"

He started to make sudden, unpredictable turns, zooming through the streets of the city, but the cops stayed on his tail. The driver turned another corner. Momentarily out of the cops' sight, he immediately veered into a narrow, dark alley. The police raced past the alley, continuing down the street.

Thinking they had escaped, the criminals breathed a sigh of relief. But then, from the other end of the alley, another cop car headed straight at them!

"Oh man!" the first guy in the construction disguise cried. "It's over!"

"Superfly's gonna kill us!" the driver moaned.

As the police car drove right toward them, they were suddenly lifted off the ground and into the sky, ice cream truck and all! "*AAAAHHHH!*" the criminals inside screamed as the truck banged and scraped against the sides of buildings.

"What kind of ice cream truck you got here?!" the second construction guy yelled.

"This isn't my truck doing this!" the driver shouted back. "Something's lifting us!"

"What?" the first construction guy screamed.

"I have no idea!" the driver admitted.

Inside a skyscraper, a businessman struggled to get an ice cream bar out of a broken vending machine. *CRASH!* The ice cream truck smashed through the wall, knocking ice cream bars out of the vending machine and scattering them all over the floor. The employee jumped out of the way, shocked, then started eagerly scooping up ice cream bars.

Inside the truck, the criminals were tossed around like shirts in a dryer as the vehicle continued to be carried. The stolen device also tumbled violently, until it started to shoot off sparks.

Past the Statue of Liberty, over Staten Island, whatever or whoever was carrying the ice cream truck through the air dropped it in a yard full of wrecked boats. *WHAM!* The truck landed on top of a decrepit freighter.

As the criminals inside scrambled to their feet, something tore the back door off the truck. *CROOONCH!*

The crooks couldn't believe what they saw. Recoiling in fear, the first construction guy said, "Is that . . . ?"

Trembling, the driver stammered, "He's—he's a . . ."

"You really are . . . ," the second construction guy muttered.

"Superfly," the mutant said, finishing their sentences.

In the laboratory at T.C.R.I. headquarters, Cynthia Utrom watched as scientists failed to mutate a hippopotamus. "Disappointing," she said, frowning.

"Yes," her head scientist agreed. "We still have been completely unable to replicate Stockman's formula. I guess we'll try another formulation. And get another hippo."

Spider strode into the lab. "It happened again," he reported. "One of our trucks got hit. They stole a radioactive storage unit this time." He pointed to a screen on the wall. It showed news footage of the ice cream truck flying away. The caption read, "SUPERFLY STRIKES AGAIN!"

Utrom's eyes narrowed. "Put tracking devices on all our deliverables. It's time we met this . . . Superfly."

Splinter finally allowed his four sons to venture out of the sewers again. For one thing, he needed them to go fetch his favorite snacks.

They stood on the roof of a tall building, shooting funny videos for their own amusement. Raph held a *katana*—a long martial arts sword—in his hands, waggling it over his shoulder like a baseball bat. "Lob it up!" he urged. "Lob it up!"

"Stay still!" Mikey said, hefting a watermelon in both hands. "We've got to keep you in the frame. Okay, ready?"

"Totally," Raph said.

Mikey lobbed the watermelon at him. *SHHHWOOMP!*

Raph sliced the melon in half, midair.

When they watched the video, the Turtles were thrilled. "Ohhhhhh!" they exclaimed. "Oh, that's amazing!"

On Leo's phone, a text popped in from Splinter: REMEMBER! NO SHENANIGANS! COME RIGHT HOME!

"Come on, guys," Leo said to his brothers. "We *just* got ungrounded. Let's go home."

But Donnie ignored him, looking at his own phone. "Yo! Check it out in slo-mo!" Mikey and Raph leaned in to stare at the screen. Slicing the watermelon looked even more awesome in slow motion!

"Let's try it again with ninja stars!" Raph suggested.

Moments later, Raph held a throwing star in his hand, ready to toss it into a watermelon held by Mikey. "Okay, eye of the tiger," Raph told himself. "Nice and easy."

"Guys?" Mikey asked nervously. "Do I have to be the one to hold the melon?"

"Who else is gonna do it, Mikey?" Raph asked.

Donatello made a reassuring face, as if having ninja stars thrown your way was no big deal. "Don't worry about it, Mikey. You're fine. Chill!" Donnie turned to Leo and joked, "He's gonna die."

"I got this!" Raph protested, having overheard Donnie. "Come on, guys!"

"Just be aware of the wind, okay?" Leo cautioned. "Gotta compensate."

"The only wind is coming from your mouth!" Raph jeered.

Mikey looked at the watermelon he was holding up and realized something. "Hey, why did we pick a fruit shaped exactly like my head?"

Raph scowled. "Stop talking! It's ruining my concentration."

Cupping his hand to his mouth, Donnie called to Mikey, "Don't worry; I've got bandages on standby just in case. You're good."

"Thanks," Mikey said a little uncertainly.

"All right," Raph said, raising his throwing arm. "One, two, three . . . *HEEYAH!*" He whipped the pointed star at the watermelon.

Mikey couldn't help but scream. *"AAHHH!"*

SHHHWOOK! The star sliced right through the watermelon and sailed over the edge of the roof.

"OW!" a voice cried below.

"Did you hear that?" Leo asked, concerned. "What *was* that?" The four brothers rushed to the side and peered over. Down on the street, a teenage girl had the ninja star stuck in her scooter helmet. She was okay but obviously angry.

"Hey!" she shouted up at the Turtles, pointing at them accusingly. "You on the roof! You reckless lunatics! I see you! Don't try to hide! You hit me in the head with a ninja star! What do you idiots think you're doing up there?!"

Raph frowned. "What's *her* deal?"

"She's yelling at us a *lot*," Donnie noted.

Mikey had a theory. "I think she's mad that we hit her with a ninja star."

While he watched the girl shouting and gesturing, Leo felt as if time had slowed down, and everything was happening in slow motion. To him, the girl looked beautiful. "Hey, maybe we should go down and talk to her," he suggested, trying to sound nonchalant. "You know, just to check on her? To make sure she's okay."

The girl could see them talking among themselves.

"No, don't sidebar! This is one of the most populated cities on planet Earth, all right? You can't just be running around recklessly with weapons! That's dangerous!"

While she was busy yelling at the Turtles, a dude in a hoodie walked up behind her.

"I think that guy is helping her," Mikey observed.

"I think he's stealing her scooter!" Leo said.

Mikey realized his brother was right. He shouted down to the teenage girl. "Hey! Lady! Behind you!"

This made the girl even angrier. "Hey! No! Why are you yelling at me? I'm the one who got hit with a ninja star!"

Leo tried to warn her. "Mysterious figure! Taking your scooter!"

"You owe me money!" the girl yelled, holding up her helmet. "These helmets aren't free!"

"No, your scooter!" Leo called.

Finally, the girl turned around. Sure enough, the dude in the hoodie was making off with her scooter. "Hey!" she shrieked at him. "What are you doing?! HEY!" The guy rode off, taking her backpack, too. When she started to run after him, a driver honked his horn at her.

"Don't honk at me!" she yelled, pointing. "Honk at him!"

Up on the roof, Raph turned away, shrugging. "Well, we tried to warn her. Nothing more we can do. You guys want to get pizza or—"

"No!" Leo interrupted. "She got her scooter stolen, and it's our fault! We have to fix this!"

"Yeah, man, that sucks," Donnie said, "but *do* we have to fix this? I mean, technically, she was just in the wrong place at the wrong time. It's not really our fault . . ."

But Leonardo's eyes were wide with determination. He felt as though he suddenly had only one mission in life. "I gotta get the scooter back to this beautiful and charming human woman!"

Leo turned to his brothers. "Alpha formation! GO!" Then he jumped off the roof and chased after the scooter thief.

"He's gone rogue!" Raph exclaimed. "I've gotta help him!"

"Whoa!" Donnie yelled.

"He just jumped off the edge," Mikey uttered in disbelief.

Seeing no other choice, the three brothers followed Leo down to the street and ran after him and the thief. Soon they'd caught up with their leader.

The thief drove into a large garage. Not an honest garage but a chop shop where crooks broke down stolen vehicles—cars, motorcycles, scooters—to sell their parts for cash. Outside the building, Leo huddled with his brothers, making a plan. "All right, guys. Guard the exits. We're gonna need the most foolproof plan. Every single ninja technique. I need you to use stealth to block the doors."

But Raph wasn't interested in stealth. "Oh, did you say go in LOUD?" Wielding his sai, he burst through the front door whooping. *"WHOOOO! WHOOO!"* Donnie, Mikey, and Leo had no choice but to follow him.

Once inside the chop shop, Raph found himself staring down a bunch of very tough-looking thieves. "Whooo?" he said, quickly losing enthusiasm for a fight.

"That's a lot of guys," Leo hissed. "They look really mean."

The crooks were pretty surprised to see four human-sized Turtles, brandishing martial arts weapons, burst through their front door. "What the heck are those things?" one dude asked, baffled.

Another guy squinted at the Turtles. "I think they're those guys who work in Times Square. You know, the mascots? Walking around in costumes, posing for pictures, shaking down the tourists for cash. It oughta be illegal!" He finished pulling the catalytic converter out of a stolen car.

"This is fine," Leo reassured his brothers quietly. "You know, we've prepared our whole lives for this." But he didn't truly believe what he was saying. He gulped, freaked out at being surrounded by menacing humans.

"We've never been in an actual fight before," Donnie whispered. "And I don't know if you've noticed, but all I've got is a big stick." He held up his bo staff. "How did I end up with the big stick?!"

Mikey held up a finger. "I know! How about we defuse this awkward situation with laughter?" He took a step toward the thieves. "Mahh wife!" he said, imitating a goofy character in a comedy movie he'd seen.

"Never been in a fight? Speak for yourself!" Raph told Donnie. "I dream about fighting every night!"

Donnie put a hand on his shoulder. "Face it, Raph. You've got a rage problem."

"It's not a problem!" Raph yelled. *"WHOOOO!"* He charged right at the tough guys, but he slipped in a puddle of motor oil, flew into the air, and slammed onto the ground. *WHOMP!* One sai fell out of his hand and into Donnie's leg.

"Rogue sai!" Leo shouted.

"YAHHHHH!" Donnie screamed.

"I think I'm gonna be sick," Leo confessed, staring at his punctured brother.

Mikey groaned, feeling woozy at the sight of the sai stuck in Donatello's leg. "Leo? What happened? Is Donnie bleeding?"

"It's still in my leg!" Donnie screamed.

"Mikey, watch out!" Leo yelled.

Too late. A fire extinguisher, tossed by one of the thieves, whizzed through the air and smacked Mikey in the back of the head. *CLANK!* He fell to the floor.

"We're not off to a great start here, guys," Leo said.

From the floor, Mikey said, "Maybe they'll see the humanity in our tragic backstory."

But the crooks had heard enough out of the Turtles. "MURDER THE FREAKS!" one of them bellowed.

Mikey desperately tried one more attempt at charming them with humor. "Mahh wife?"

Unamused, the tough guys charged right at the

Turtles. Raph picked up Leo. "Think fast, Leo!"

"Hey, what are you doing?!" Leo protested. "No! Stop!"

Using all his strength, Raph lifted Leo over his head and threw him at the thief leading the charge. Leo managed to land a flying kick in the guy's face, sending him sprawling!

"Whoo-hoo!" Raph cheered.

Scrambling to his feet, Leo said, "All right, Raph. You go left. I'll go—"

But Raph ignored him and did his own thing. Leo got knocked down.

"What the heck, man?!" Leo cried. "I said go left!"

"I got him!" Raph replied, taking down an attacker.

As more humans came at them, Raph got hit from behind. Leo spotted a big dude rushing toward Michelangelo. "Mikey, watch out!" Leo warned.

Mikey ran and slid over the hood of a car being dismantled for parts. He tried to climb inside the car, but the door was locked. As he tugged on the door handle, a hulking brute swung a crowbar at him. Mikey dodged the blow. *SMASH!* One of the car's passenger windows splintered into pieces.

"Oh snap!" Mikey cried. "Weave, weave!"

Surrounded by foes, Mikey threw his body into the air, backflipped over the attackers, and crashed through the car's sun roof. *CRASH!* From the inside, he unlocked the door, popped out, and escaped across the room, passing Donnie. The humans chased after him, but Donnie confronted them with his bo staff.

"Back off!" he said, twirling the staff. "I've got a big stick!"

Mikey grabbed a wrench off a workbench and threw it at the closest crook, who held a gun in his hand. *BLAM!* The gun went off, firing a bullet into the ceiling. Sparks flew from the impact, dropping onto flammable liquids.

A fire broke out!

"What do we do?" Donnie squeaked. "What do we do?!"

Mikey remembered the fire extinguisher that had smacked him in the back of the head. He spotted it on the floor, under a table. Stooping quickly, he grabbed the extinguisher, pulled its pin, and started spraying foam at the spreading flames. *WHOOSH!*

But then one of the thieves jumped into a car and started the engine. *VRRRROOOM!* He aimed the headlights right at the Turtles.

"Uh-oh," Mikey said.

The car roared straight toward the brothers, but they leapt and spun out of the way. Donnie grabbed a pole and tossed it like a spear through the open driver's window. It jammed the steering wheel, locking the car into a hard right turn. The car spun around and around in a circle in the middle of the shop floor. The Turtles were stuck in the middle of the circle.

"He's doing doughnuts around us!" Donnie shouted.

Springing into action, Raph hopped onto the roof of the car, reached in through the open sunroof, and popped the car into neutral. It spun to a stop, and the driver stumbled out, dizzy from all the spins. Groaning and clutching his head, he fell to the floor.

"I'm awesome," Raph said immodestly.

"Guys, look around!" Donnie said.

They saw they'd knocked all the thieves to the floor. Their first battle was over, and the Turtles had won!

"WHOOOO!" Raph whooped.

"Did you see that?!" Leo crowed.

"I totally helped!" Mikey shouted joyfully.

Suddenly the chop shop's garage door opened. Light poured in. The Turtles whipped around to see who they would face next.

"Hide! Hide!" Donnie whispered. Remembering that they really weren't supposed to let humans see them, the brothers scattered, ducking down behind cars.

The girl they'd seen from the roof strode into the chop shop, walking right past all the crooks on the floor and straight to her scooter. "Wow," she said, grabbing its handlebars. "My scooter's okay. That's good."

Then she looked around, finally noticing all the defeated thieves. "Whoa! This is crazy!"

She peered into the shadows where the Turtles were hiding. "Hey! I see you in there!"

"Guys, I think she can see us," Mikey whispered.

"She can totally see us," Donnie whispered back.

"Come on out!" the girl urged. "Come on! I won't make a big deal about the ninja star. You got my scooter back, so we're square."

The Turtles stayed put. They'd never talked to a human before. And hadn't their father warned them that humans were the demon scum of the earth?

Leo leaned toward Donnie. "You go out first," he whispered. "You're the most inviting and friendly."

"The longer you lurk in the shadows," the girl told them, "the more sus it gets every second. Come out and say hi. I'm April O'Neil, by the way."

"She said we're sus!" Donnie whispered. "That's not good! That is not good!"

"Sus. Right," Mikey said. "Um, what's sus?"

"Like suspicious," Raph explained.

"Yeah, and now it's like doubly sus to be whispering about how sus you are," April said.

Freaked out, Leo tried to hold his brothers back, but Raph, Donnie, and Mikey stepped forward. "Wassup?" Donnie said.

"Hey," Mikey said shyly.

April stared at the Turtles. "Whoa. Are those your costumes? You're crime fighters with turtle costumes?! Weird! Not sure I follow the thinking." She ran up and grabbed Leo's arm. "The sleeve feels totally real! What is that, some kind of silicone? These costumes look really expensive!"

"That's my skin," Leo explained.

"That's your . . . skin," April said slowly, taking in this information. "What in the universe *are* you guys?!"

The Turtles looked at each other, unsure what to say. Where to start with their story? How far back should they go? And would April believe them, anyway?

Mikey stepped forward. "Can we explain this over some pizza?"

April thought it over. "How you guys feel about pepperoni?"

A little while later, the Turtles and April sat on a rooftop eating pizza together. After introducing themselves, the Turtles all tried to explain their unusual origin, interrupting and speaking over each other. Finally, April held her hands up, gesturing for silence.

"Stop, stop, stop!" April said. "Let me see if I've got this right. You were real turtles, but you got dipped in some mystery ooze and got turned into mutant turtle men?"

"Turtle boys, actually," Mikey corrected her.

"I would say teens," Leo said. "Like cool teenagers."

April wrote this information down in a notebook. "Amazing. Tell me more! I want to know everything about you. Are there more of you?"

"No, just us," Donnie said, his mouth full of pizza.

"They are alone in this world," April said out loud as

she wrote the words. She looked up from her notebook. "And nobody's ever asked you about this or talked to you about this?"

The Turtles shook their heads. "Nope."

"No."

"You're the first one."

"People should talk to us!"

April smiled. She had a terrific idea. . . .

April put down her notebook and spoke excitedly to the four Turtles. "Look, I write for my school paper, and I *was* writing this story on Superfly and his mysterious string of super crimes. Don't steal that, by the way. That's *my* phrase. But this! Turtle mutant karate teens! This is *way* better! This will get me a TV show! They could call it *Good Night, April* or *April Tonight.* Do you get what I'm saying?"

The Turtles looked at each other, overwhelmed by April's enthusiasm. "Look," Raph said, "I don't know if we should cooperate with your story."

April looked shocked. To her, the idea was a slam dunk. "Why not?" she asked. "This is *gold*!"

Donnie tried to explain their hesitation. "We were taught that humans would try to destroy us if they ever found out we existed. Kill us! Put us in a zoo!"

April shrugged this off. "Well, I won't do that! I don't even own a zoo!"

"Look, April," Mikey said. "I got a question, so just be straight with me. Do you think there are more like you? People who will accept us?"

There was a heavy pause while the Turtles anxiously awaited her answer. Then April, deciding to be completely open and honest with her new acquaintances, said, "No. Absolutely not. I mean, like, really. No."

The Turtles hung their heads, looking down at the roof they were sitting on, disappointed.

"Splinter was right," Leo said.

"I knew it," Raph said.

"If I'm being honest," April continued, "the reason I'm not scared of you is that you helped me out. If you hadn't, and I had just stumbled across you, the sight of you four would totally freak me out." Her phone vibrated. "My mom is texting."

Donnie held up his phone. "Dad's texting me! He's

freaking out a bit."

April grinned. "Guess all parents are the same, huh?"

"One hundred percent," Leo said a little too quickly.

"Yeah, for sure," Mikey said a little too loudly.

"Our dad is definitely not a giant rat!" Donnie exclaimed.

April gave Donnie a questioning look. "That makes me feel like he's a rat. Well, I'll air-drop you my contact info. If you ever feel like you can come out into the world, let me know. I'd love to write the story about it. Seriously. Good night." She opened a door and headed confidently down the dusty steps. The Turtles watched her go.

"She seemed cool," Leo said, infatuated.

"Here he goes again," Mikey said. "That's your type?"

"Every girl, man . . . ," Donnie said, shaking his head.

Leo acted like he wasn't at all interested in April. "I'm not even that into her." Then he turned to Donnie. "Give me that contact info!"

As they made their way home through the sewers, the Turtles discussed their amazing victory over the chop shop thieves and their encounter with April. "My mind is just blown!" Mikey enthused. "A human! We talked to a human!"

"And we also punched and kicked and headbutted them!" Raph reminded him.

Donnie held up his bo staff, marveling. "The stick! The stick worked!"

"I want *more,* guys!" Mikey confessed. "I got the taste of life and don't want to wash it out of my mouth! I want it to linger on my tongue, swish around my throat."

"You're really driving that image into the ground, man," Donnie said.

"But he's right!" Raph said. "It was too good to give up on!"

Out in front, Leo spun around and walked backward, addressing his brothers. "But you guys heard April and the words that came out of her incredibly formed and beautiful mouth. The only reason she liked us was because we saved her. She saw us as heroes."

Donnie got an idea. "So what if *everyone* saw us as heroes?"

Mikey looked confused. "What do you mean?"

"I mean, look!" Donnie said, pointing up through a

sewer grate. On the side of a building, a huge screen was showing the news. The headline read, "SUPERFLY CRIME SYNDICATE PULLS OFF ICE CREAM TRUCK CAPER IN MANHATTAN."

Leo, Raph, and Mikey read the headline, then looked at Donnie curiously. They still didn't understand what he was trying to say. What did some crooks have to do with them getting to experience more of the world outside the sewers?

"Don't you get it?" he asked excitedly. "We'll use our ninja skills to take out Superfly!"

Donnie kept talking, painting a vivid picture of how their heroic triumph was going to go down. He could picture the whole thing in his mind. “First, we’ll track this Superfly dude down. Then we’ll drag him to city hall, dump him on the steps for the cops, and say, ‘We’re the heroes who stopped Superfly. Yeah, we look a little different, but we’re on your side!’ And everyone will be like, ‘Hey, those Turtles are all right! I’m a cabbie from da Bronx!’” Donnie delivered those last two lines in a pretty terrible New York accent. “Then everyone in the city will know we’re cool! They’ll accept us!”

Mikey beamed, totally on board with Donnie’s plan.

"Yeah," he said dreamily, imagining how it would be. "And our fans will, like, ask us to autograph their babies!"

Donnie wasn't sure about that detail, but he continued with his vision of how life would change for the Turtles. "Then, once the overall fanfare has settled down, we'll enroll in high school, where we'll be normal if not slightly-more-popular-than-average students!"

Raphael nodded. "This is a great plan! If this works, I won't have to hang with you losers for the rest of my life!"

"That's very true!" Donnie agreed.

"What about Dad, though?" Mikey asked.

Donnie considered this. Mikey had a point. Splinter would never agree to them running around the city chasing Superfly. "I mean, he doesn't really need to know about it, right?"

Donnie, Mikey, and Raph all turned to Leo. When it came to keeping secrets from their dad, he'd thrown them under the bus before. Would he agree to Donnie's scheme for acceptance and popularity?

"Look," Leo said. "If we're going to do this, we're going to have to get April's help. Sounds like she's been doing tons of research on Superfly. She probably has some good leads."

Raph's eyes bulged. "Whoa, whoa, whoa, whoa, whoa. Whoa. So you're *in*?!"

Smiling and nodding, Leo said, "Yeah, I'm in!"

The brothers bumped fists and high-fived. "Yeahhhh!"

"So," Raph asked, "where do we start?"

Leo pulled out his phone and pressed the call button.

On the subway, April felt her phone vibrate. She pulled it out of her pocket and looked at the screen to see who was calling. Then she answered it. "Turtle . . . fellas? Is this you?"

"Hi, April," Leo said into his phone. "It's Leo, one of the . . . Turtle fellas. So, uh, we have a proposal."

"Okay," April said.

"You help us find Superfly," Leo continued, "and we bring him to justice. You document it all. When we get him, you release the story. You become a famous reporter, and we get accepted by the world as heroes.

What do you think? Is it a deal?"

All the guys were gathered around Leo's phone, eagerly awaiting April's response.

"Wow! YES!" they heard her say. "Amazing!" Then April felt as though she was revealing a little bit *too* much enthusiasm and decided to play it cool. "If I'm being honest, I totally stopped even thinking about this," she said. "I had a lot of things to do."

That was a fib. If the Turtles had been able to see April's notebook at that moment, they'd have seen that it was covered in notes about them, like "Who are the turtle boys?!" and "Sewers?"

"By the way," she asked curiously, "do you guys have ears?"

"Just say yes, just say yes," Mikey urged quietly.

"I think so?" Leo answered.

"They think they have ears," April said out loud as she wrote in her notebook. "Okay, perfect. Yes. Meet me at Eastman High tomorrow night at eight p.m. Everyone will be gone. I have all my research in the school newspaper's office."

"Cool, cool," Leo said, trying to act calm and indifferent,

even though his heart was pounding. “So, uh, it’s a date.”

“What?!” Donnie whispered.

“No!” Mikey whispered.

“I mean, uh . . . ,” Leo stammered.

“Just hang up, man!” Raph whispered.

“It’s not a date, uh . . . ,” Leo said lamely.

“You’re making it worse!” Donnie hissed.

“Uh, bad service,” Leo improvised, making static sounds. “I’ll see ya tomorrow.” He hung up and turned to his brothers, smiling. “Not bad, huh?”

The other three rolled their eyes and winced.

The next evening, the Turtles headed out of their quarters and into the sewer. Splinter watched them go. “So you go to store, steal food, and come back? That’s *it*! Right?”

“Yep!” Mikey fibbed.

“Of course!” Raph said at the same time.

“Back before you know it,” Donnie assured their dad, trying to sound casual.

The three of them looked at Leo, waiting for him to

chime in and back them up in their small bending of the truth. He hated lying to his father, but he wanted to be loyal to his brothers. Besides, he really wanted to see April again, and Splinter would never let that happen.

"Yeah," Leo said. "To the store and right back."

The four of them filed out quickly.

Splinter narrowed his gaze suspiciously. He could sense when his adopted sons were lying. "They are up to something," he muttered to himself.

Once they emerged from the sewers, the Turtles took to the rooftops of New York to avoid the gaze of humans. They hopped from the top of one building to the next until they reached a structure next to Eastman High School. Peering over a ledge, they saw April holding a back door open. She was waiting for them.

"Hey!" Leo called down to her, waving.

April looked up and saw the four Turtles leaning over the edge of the roof. Smiling, she waved back and motioned for them to hurry to the ground. The brothers scrambled down the building's fire escape and landed in the dark alleyway next to the high school's back entrance.

"Hey! You made it!" April greeted them. She

gestured up toward the roof where she'd seen them. "That seemed very dangerous."

"That? Ha! Not at all," Leo boasted, waving her concern away. "We eat danger for breakfast."

"Actually, I eat pizza with bits of waffle on it," Mikey clarified. April raised her eyebrows.

"It's better than it sounds," Donnie said, defending his brother's breakfast choice.

"It actually sounds delicious, if I'm being honest," April said. She held the back door open wide. "Come on in."

The Turtles hesitated. Now that they finally had the opportunity to walk into an actual high school, they weren't sure they deserved such an honor. "Really?" Mikey asked. "We can just go in there?"

"Of course!" April said. To her, going inside the high school was no big deal, something she did every day. She ushered the guys into the empty hallway, closed the door behind them, and opened her arms wide. "Welcome to Eastman High."

Awestruck, the Turtles looked around, almost afraid to speak, as if they were in a sacred space. "Wow . . . ," Donnie said, his eyes wide. With April leading the way, they started to stroll down the hall.

April was amazed by their reactions to being in the building. "This is very strange. I can't believe you guys actually *want* to go to high school." There were many days when April would've much preferred to be out on the streets of the city chasing down the facts of a hot new story instead of sitting in a stuffy classroom.

"Yeah, we do!" Raph said enthusiastically. "We *very* much do! Don't you love high school?"

April's eyes darted around a bit. "Yes," she answered a bit woodenly. "As a very popular and well-liked person, I *love* high school." She seemed to want to change the subject. "But don't worry about me. Is this living up to your dreams?"

"No," Donnie said. "It's even better!" He spotted a sticker on a locker. "One Punch Man! Whoever's locker this is likes anime! I don't even know this person, and they get me more than anyone ever has!"

"Guys, look!" Mikey cried, running over to a poster that read IMPROV TEAM TRYOUTS. "I've gotta sign up. This is amazing!"

Leo pulled Mikey away from the poster, which he

was practically hugging. "Mikey, what are you doing? We don't even go here!"

"Yet," Mikey countered. "The tryouts aren't for two weeks. We could be enrolled by then!" He squinted at the poster, reading the fine print at the bottom. "They need a last name. Wait, what's our last name?"

Leo looked puzzled. "I've never really thought about that. . . ."

"Do we not have last names?" Raph asked.

"Who *are* we?" Donnie pondered.

"It's okay!" Mikey said, grabbing the pencil attached to a string and writing on the sign-up sheet. "I'll just break it up. Michael Angelo." He used a bad Italian accent. "Heyyy! I'm Michael Angelo! Perfecto!"

"Ha!" Raph laughed, pointing at Leo. "That makes you Leo Nardo!"

"NARDOOOO!" Donnie said, loving the sound of it.

"I am *not* Nardo!" Leo insisted.

April tried to intervene. "Guys! Lay off Nardo! He's sensitive! Come on. The office is this way." Leo didn't like her calling him Nardo, but he loved her coming to his defense.

"Ha ha!" Mikey laughed. "She called him Nardo, too!"

"Nardo!" Donnie repeated.

April led them to the school newspaper's office. Inside, they passed on into a small, dark room. "The newspaper and yearbook staffers used to use this as a darkroom, back when they had to develop pictures. But since everything went digital, nobody uses it anymore. So I set up my investigative materials in here."

April switched on a light, and the Turtles saw a big corkboard with materials related to Superfly tacked to it. There were newspaper clippings about crimes. Mug shots. Photos of a pro wrestler named Jimmy "Superfly" Snuka. A poster for the 1972 movie *Superfly.* In the middle of the board was a card that read, "WHO IS SUPERFLY?" Strings connected all the pictures and articles pinned to the board.

"WHOAAA!" the Turtles exclaimed when they saw the elaborate display. April had really done her homework!

"Yeah, that's right," April said proudly with her arms folded across her chest. "My board is incredibly impressive."

She slowly wandered the room, tenting her fingers and touching them to her chin. "Okay, here's what I got. Superfly seems to be building something. Something big, powerful, and deadly. He's stealing some insanely high-tech, cutting-edge equipment. State of the art. Incredibly expensive. He pays off thieves to do his dirty work so he can stay completely under the radar. Nobody's ever seen his face."

"Why?" Mikey asked.

"Because he kills everyone who does!" April replied.

"Whooaaa," all four Turtles said together. "Cool!"

"No," April said, shaking her head. "Not cool."

"A bit cool," Raph suggested.

Leo decided to change the subject and get down to business. "So how are we gonna find this Superfly?" He studied April's board but didn't see any information about Superfly's whereabouts.

Joining him at her case board, April pointed to a mug shot of a slender guy glaring into the camera. "See this guy? That's Skinny Sam. He was in on the ice cream truck heist last week."

"Ice cream truck heist?" Mikey repeated. "Sounds delicious."

"Like on the news report we saw," Donnie said. "Remember?"

Mikey said, "Nope."

"The thieves used an ice cream truck to steal a radioactive storage unit," April explained. "And look! I found *this* at that chop shop where the dude took my scooter." She held up a diagram of a complex-looking device.

Mikey studied it carefully, nodding wisely. "A drawing. Interesting . . ."

"Not just a drawing," April said. "A diagram of a

radioactive storage unit exactly like the one Superfly's crew stole!"

"I get it!" Donnie said. "You think there's a connection between Superfly and those guys we fought in the chop shop."

"Fought *and* defeated," Raph added.

Donnie pointed his finger at Raph and made a clicking sound with his tongue, acknowledging his brother's correction.

"Bingo," April said. She gestured toward mug shots on her case board. "These are pictures of the crooks running that chop shop. They must be doing business for Superfly." Pointing at four photos one by one, she said, "Fat Frank, Bald Bronson, Toupee Tom, and Normal Nate." Each guy's appearance matched his nickname perfectly. "They can lead us to Superfly."

Leo smiled confidently. "That's a lot of leads."

"And a lot of appearance-based nicknames," Mikey observed.

"Luckily, we got a lot of fists," Raph said, holding his up.

"Let's start chasing them down," April said.

And so they began their quest to stop the mysterious

criminal known as Superfly. Using April's notes, they snuck out at night and headed to the locations all over the city where the crooks connected to the chop shop were known to hang out.

Outside a gambling den, the Turtles flew into action, using their ninja skills to defeat thieves and gangsters.

At another chop shop, they honed their skills on live humans, whirling their swords, sai, nunchucks, and bo staff to great effect.

As another criminal came out the back door of an illegal club into a dark alley, he was astonished to find himself set upon by four human-sized Turtles whirling, punching, and kicking. One of them even seemed to be recording the action on his phone!

Cops found brutes wanted for dozens of crimes tied up outside their police stations, neatly delivered like birthday packages. As the officers hauled the crooks inside to be arrested and jailed, April watched from across the street, furiously typing details into her laptop.

Later, she and the Turtles whooped and laughed, watching videos on their phones of the brothers tackling bad guys and besting them. Their martial arts skills were getting sharper and sharper!

Feeling confident that they'd soon be allowed to go to high school, the guys tried on new school outfits. "Does this look cool?" Raph asked, squeezing into a brightly colored shirt.

"Yes," Mikey said, "if by *cool,* you mean 'trying way too hard to be cool.'"

Raph scoffed. "Says the guy in a Hawaiian shirt."

Donnie and Leo were pleased with their outfits. "This is a lot, but I think I can pull it off," Donnie remarked.

"Not bad," Leo said, admiring himself in a broken mirror they'd hauled back from a trash bin. He had on khakis and a short-sleeved shirt.

"You look like you work at an appliance store," Donnie teased.

"You say that like it's a bad thing," Leo countered.

For research on how to behave once they got to high school, they watched more movies starring good-looking teenagers.

Eager to make faster progress in their pursuit of Superfly, the Turtles started sneaking out in the middle of the afternoon when their dad was taking his nap. But as they crept out of their quarters, Splinter stealthily opened one eye, watching them go. . . .

They even dared sneaking back to Eastman High School to peer through the windows and spy on April. They saw her being congratulated on her latest article in the school paper: "Mysterious Vigilantes Take On Superfly!"

Splinter tried to catch the Turtles scheming in their bedroom, but when he yanked back the curtain in their doorway, they were lying on their beds innocently pretending to read. All the evidence of their crime-busting outings—and their high school outfits—was carefully hidden underneath their beds.

Eventually, they managed to catch up with Fat Frank. But when they questioned him, he said, "Bald Bronson deals with all that stuff! I'm just a numbers guy!"

So they found Bald Bronson and persuaded him to talk. But all he said was "I don't know nothing about Superfly! Normal Nate said he was planning some sort of heist for him, though. . . ."

It took some doing, but they managed to track down Normal Nate, who told the Turtles, "Yeah, that wasn't me—that was Toupee Tom. Bald Bronson always gets us mixed up!"

When they finally cornered Toupee Tom, they were in for yet another disappointment. "Yeah, I was planning a heist, but Bad Bernie is the one behind it all! He took over the whole operation. Bad Bernie is who you want!"

Raph was growing impatient with all these dead ends. "And where do we find BAD BERNIE?!" he bellowed, getting right in Toupee Tom's face.

Terrified by the mutants, Toupee Tom blurted out a list of Bad Bernie's favorite hangouts. The Turtles visited them one by one, finally catching up with Bad Bernie at the last place on the list, a grimy old pool hall. Using their honed ninja skills, they quickly tied the criminal up, refusing to let him go until he told them what they wanted to know.

"Okay, okay!" Bad Bernie moaned. "I'll talk!"

"We're listening," Leo said.

"And remembering," Mikey said. "Without even taking notes."

Donnie held up his phone, open to a note-taking app. "Actually, I *am* taking notes."

Bad Bernie made a pained expression, as if it hurt him to give up information. But then he said in a gravelly voice, "My guys got hired by Superfly and his crew to steal this radioactive storage unit. We pulled it off, so he hired us for another job. He's building something big and messed up. Anyway, he just needs one more thing: an assimilator. Industrial, large-scale, hard to come by. But we got a tip as to where we might find such an item."

He described going with his crew to the docks the night before. They knocked out guards and stole an assimilator from a shipping container.

Bad Bernie proudly smiled, remembering. "It was ripe for the taking. So we took it. And tonight at ten o'clock, we're gonna hand it over to Superfly under the bridge. Nice and smooth."

The Turtles wasted no time in taking this information to April. "The way I see it," Raph said excitedly, "we'll take out Bad Bernie's crew, switch places with them, and Superfly will get caught in our web. BOOM!"

"Man, I wish I'd been there for Bad Bernie's

confession," April said. "It would've made some great video."

"No problem," Donnie said. "Get your camera ready. I can be Bad Bernie, easy." He started talking in his terrible New York accent. "I'm a gangster! But dees toitles are too tough for me! Fuhgeddaboudit! I'm gonna spill da beans! Just tell me what youse wanna know. Maybe youse wanna know all about dis Superfly?"

April just shook her head. "Um, I thought you wanted people to *like* you."

Donnie's phone went off, sounding like a warning alarm. "Uh-oh, text from Dad." He held it up for everyone to see: BOYS! EMERGENCY! COME HOME!

April walked with the Turtles through a sewer tunnel. "What do you think is wrong?" she asked as they hurried along.

"I bet that cat is back," Donnie speculated. "He freaks out every time!"

"Hopefully it's nothing, and we can head straight to the docks and meet up with Superfly!" Leo said. He came to a stop. "All right, April," he said, pointing farther along the tunnel. "We live just up there. But our dad doesn't really like humans, so . . ." He paused, hoping

April would understand that they couldn't take her any farther into their world.

"Rude," April said. "But to be fair, I don't love rats."

"And that's totally fair!" Leo told her.

"Understandable," Raph said, nodding. "Just wait here. We'll be back in a few."

The Turtles headed on up the tunnel and into their living quarters. Everything was dark.

"Dad . . . ?" Leo said.

The lights snapped on. "SURPRISE!" Splinter yelled.

"AHHH!" the brothers screamed, startled. But when they looked around, they saw that their father had set up a little party, complete with several pizzas. There were even balloons tied to the table.

Catching his breath, Leo gasped, "Dad, you really can't just scare us like that!"

Donnie gestured toward the table with the pizzas. "What is all this?"

"Welcome home!" Splinter said in a friendly voice.

"Why are there balloons in here?" Leo asked.

Donnie lowered his brows suspiciously. "Dad, what are you doing?"

Splinter came clean. "Look, I'm not stupid. I know something's up."

"You do?" Raph asked, looking worried.

"I do," Splinter said, nodding. "You're done with the sewers. You want to be in the human world. I went through your stuff, and I found these." He held up the clothing they'd planned to wear to high school someday.

The brothers pretended they'd never seen the outfits before. "What?" "That's not ours." "How did those even get in with our stuff?"

Splinter held up his paws. "Boys, boys," he said. "It's okay. I think I have found a way to make you happy. I have brought the human world to you!" He pulled aside a curtain, revealing cardboard cutouts of movie stars that he'd swiped from theaters. "Look! Human friends!" He moved one of the cutouts to make it look as though it were talking. "Hello! I'm a human!" He slipped on a jacket. "Watch, I'm a waiter! The full human restaurant experience! Sit down! Let me take your order. But it has to be pizza." With a sweep of his arm, he gestured for them to follow him.

The Turtles looked at the table covered with pizzas

and decorated with balloons. Then they looked at each other. "Uh, look, Dad," Leo said. "We appreciate it, but we still got more errands to run."

"Don't worry!" Splinter assured them. "You can run them later! Sit!" He hurried over to the table and pulled out a chair.

"Yeah, but they're just really important errands," Raph said.

"Oh, you know, they're urgent," Leo agreed.

"Yeah, just really, really, really important," Raph said.

Splinter stopped his waiter act and looked at his sons. "What is going on? What are you doing up there? Don't lie. Tell me. Are you in trouble? Is something wrong? Is someone trying to milk you?"

Disgusted, the Turtles shook their heads. "No!" "Ew!" "It's never milking!" "Why would somebody *do* that?!"

"Do you need help?" Splinter asked. "Anything you need, I'm here."

The brothers looked at each other again. What could they say? They didn't want to lie to their dad, but they knew he'd put a stop to their hunt for Superfly if they told him about it. And then they could kiss acceptance, and high school popularity, goodbye.

"No, we're just running errands," Leo said. "Shopping, getting the stuff we need to live down here."

"Really?" Splinter asked, looking him in the eye. "That's it?"

"Yeah," Leo said, meeting his gaze. "That is quite literally it."

"Nothing else," Raph confirmed.

The Turtles said their goodbyes and headed out. Splinter watched them go.

When the Turtles came back out of their living quarters into the sewer tunnel, April was waiting for them. She could see that they were upset. "Hey, uh, everything okay?" she asked.

The brothers kept walking past her, still thinking about how they'd just deceived their father at the very moment when he was trying to reach out to them.

"Yeah," Leo said.

"It's fine," Donnie added.

They paused and looked at each other. "Are we still sure we're doing the right thing?" Mikey asked.

Leo sighed. "Dad'll come around. And if he doesn't, after tonight it won't matter."

They headed down the tunnel, still feeling uneasy about their decision. April hurried after them, knowing something was up.

Having successfully switched places with Bad Bernie's gang, the Turtles drove their van with the assimilator in it to the Brooklyn Bridge to meet up with Superfly. Donnie took the wheel, easily navigating the streets and parking the van. Raph was impressed. "You're actually a good driver, Donnie."

"Countless hours of playing car chase video games have finally paid off!" Donnie said, grinning.

Nearby, April was filming everything. Wearing a headset, she spoke to the brothers through their earpieces. "Hey, guys."

Leo spoke into his mic. "Uh, hello, April. You there?"

"Yeah, I got you," she said. "Now just remember, this footage will be the definitive imagery of your existence. So don't make it lame or anything."

"We would have to try really hard to do that," Leo said.

Donnie pointed out the windshield. "Here he comes!"

As the Turtles watched through the windows of the van, two awesome cars and a motorcycle slowly approached the meeting point. With sleek designs, huge engines, and gleaming, colorful custom paint jobs, the vehicles were built to impress—and they succeeded.

"Look at those cars! And that bike!" Mikey said, his eyes practically popping out of his head. "This guy *is* superfly!"

"He's got some swagger to him!" Raph gushed.

"The horsepower must be crazy!" Donnie marveled.

Mikey shook his head slowly in admiration. "Look at those rims, bro!"

Leo did a quick calculation. "All right, guys. There are

two cars and a motorcycle. That means fifteen guys tops. This is gonna be a piece of cake."

Smacking one fist into his palm in happy anticipation, Raph said, "Oh man! They're gonna be so scared when they see they're about to roll up on a bunch of mutants! HA!"

One of the car doors opened. A massive dark figure emerged. As he stepped onto the ground, taking his weight off the vehicle, the car rose. The figure stepped into the light of a streetlamp, and the Turtles could see that he was a big, heavily muscled warthog man! Sporting pink hair, shades, a nose ring, and a sleeveless vest that put his bulging biceps on display, the dude was definitely intimidating.

Though the Turtles didn't know it yet, his name was Bebop.

"Uhhh . . . ," Raph said, leaving his mouth open, stunned by the sight of the guy.

"Oh, I am *so* going to win a Daytime Emmy!" April said into her earpiece.

Bebop held up an old boombox and hit Play. A song with the words *"I know I'm superfly"* blasted into the night air.

"What do we do, Leo?" Mikey squeaked.

"Uh," Leo hesitated, "I don't know. I . . ."

"Alpha formation?" Raph suggested.

Donnie turned on him. "You're not the leader! You don't even know what alpha formation is!"

Another car door opened. A monstrous foot appeared. As a creature climbed out of the car and stood in the street, the Turtles saw a giant claw. Antennae. Weird hands. Huge wings, one of which had a large chunk missing. When all these features were put together, they added up to a hulking, terrifying fly man. Superfly!

More car doors opened, and the rest of Superfly's crew emerged. Ray Fillet, a manta ray man. Genghis Frog, a frog man. Leatherhead, a crocodile woman. Rocksteady, a rhinoceros man. Mondo Gecko, a skateboarder lizard. Wingnut, a bat woman. And Scumbug, a cockroach woman. Joining Bebop, they lined up behind Superfly, facing the van.

"Yo!" Superfly yelled at the guys in the van. "Come on, y'all! Let's get the goods!"

KRRRARRNK! Superfly tore the front of the van right

off, including its windshield, revealing the four Turtles inside. *"AHHHH!"* they screamed.

"Yo!" Superfly said, surprised.

"AHHHHH!" the Turtles screamed again.

Superfly was shocked at what he saw. "WHAT?! WHAT?! Y'all some little tortoises, huh? Look at you! You're all adorable, man!" He called back to his crew, "Bad Bernie's got some turtles on the payroll!"

Leo spoke up. "No, we don't work for Bad Bernie! We're here to find you!"

Donnie was gaping at the creatures who had climbed out of the flashy cars. "I can't believe there are *other mutants.* Like *us*!"

Superfly shook his grotesque head in disbelief. "This is wild! Lemme guess. Like fifteen years ago, some sludge was dumped in a sewer, and y'all came from that. Am I right?"

Nodding, Raph said, "We prefer the term *ooze,* but yeah."

"It just sounds better," Leo added.

"*Ooze* just rolls off the tongue better," Raph said.

"Ooze," the four Turtles said in unison. "Oooozze."

"It's nice, right?" Leo asked. "It's ooze."

"Ooooze!" Superfly said, drawing out the word as though it tasted good in his fly mouth. "I like that! I like ooze. So look, look, look. That same ooze made me. My dad, Baxter Stockman, is the one who dumped that ooze down the drain. So technically, we're cousins! What up, cuz?"

"That's awesome, man!" Raph enthused.

The Turtles climbed out of what was left of the van and took a step closer, getting a better look at Superfly and his crew. "Wow!" Mikey exclaimed happily. "I've always wanted a cousin!"

"Well, look at you now. . . . You got a bunch!" Superfly laughed. "Oh, I'm so sorry. I didn't introduce my peeps!" He turned to the line of mutants and pointed at each one as he said their name. "This is Bebop and Rocksteady."

"What's going on?" Rocksteady asked. "Nice to meet you."

"A pleasure!" Bebop said.

"Right here we got Wingnut," Superfly said, continuing with his introductions.

"Hi!" Wingnut said. "Do I wave my wing or my hand?

I'll just wave both! Am I doing it right?" She waved but bumped into Bebop. "Sorry, sorry."

"We got Ray Fillet . . . ," Superfly said, pointing to the manta ray mutant.

"RAY FILLET!" the fish man shouted, lifting his arms in triumph.

"Leatherhead," Superfly went on.

"G'day, fellas!" the crocodile woman said in her Australian accent. "Nice meeting you lot!"

"Genghis Frog," Superfly said.

"Aw, look at the little jacket!" Mikey cried, pointing.

"Goochie goochie goo!" Raph said as if he were talking to a cute little baby.

Superfly pointed at the cockroach woman. "That's Scumbug. She only speaks Vermin." Making a chittering sound, Scumbag waved at the Turtles. They waved back a little uncertainly.

"And finally, Mondo Gecko," Superfly said, pointing at the lizard man.

Moving in for a hug, the spacey hippie greeted the Turtles. "What's up, bros? I'm a hugger! Get in here!" He hugged Mikey.

"You seem cool!" Mikey said. "I like your vibe!"

"I like *your* vibe!" Mondo Gecko said right back at him.

"I like *your* vibe!" Mikey repeated.

"I like *YOUR* vibe!" Mondo Gecko said.

"I like ***YOUR*** vibe!" Mikey said again.

"Digging your vibe," Mondo Gecko said, changing things up just a little.

"I like your *viiibe*!" Mikey said, drawing out the last word.

"Shh!" Leo interrupted. "Remember why we're here! The plan! April's story!"

"Oh yeah!" Mikey said, remembering.

Picking up on Leo's cue, Donnie stepped forward. "We heard you're building some sort of super weapon!"

Superfly looked offended. "Weapon?! I'm building the *opposite* of a weapon. Weapons kill. What I'm making will *create.*"

Mikey raised his eyebrows. "Okay, I'm leaning in."

Leo got right to the point. "What are you building?"

Gesturing for everyone to follow him, Superfly started walking toward a nearby bowling alley with an arcade full of games. "Yo, if we're gonna chat, let's go somewhere more fun." All his crew members and the Turtles followed the fly man.

April watched them head into the bowling alley.

LEONARDO is the leader of the Teenage Mutant Ninja Turtles. He's always ready to inspire his brothers with his confidence and hard work.

RAPHAEL is fearless and fiercely strong, and is the toughest Turtle around! He's loyal to his brothers and likes being a part of their team, but he's also excited to make friends outside the sewers.

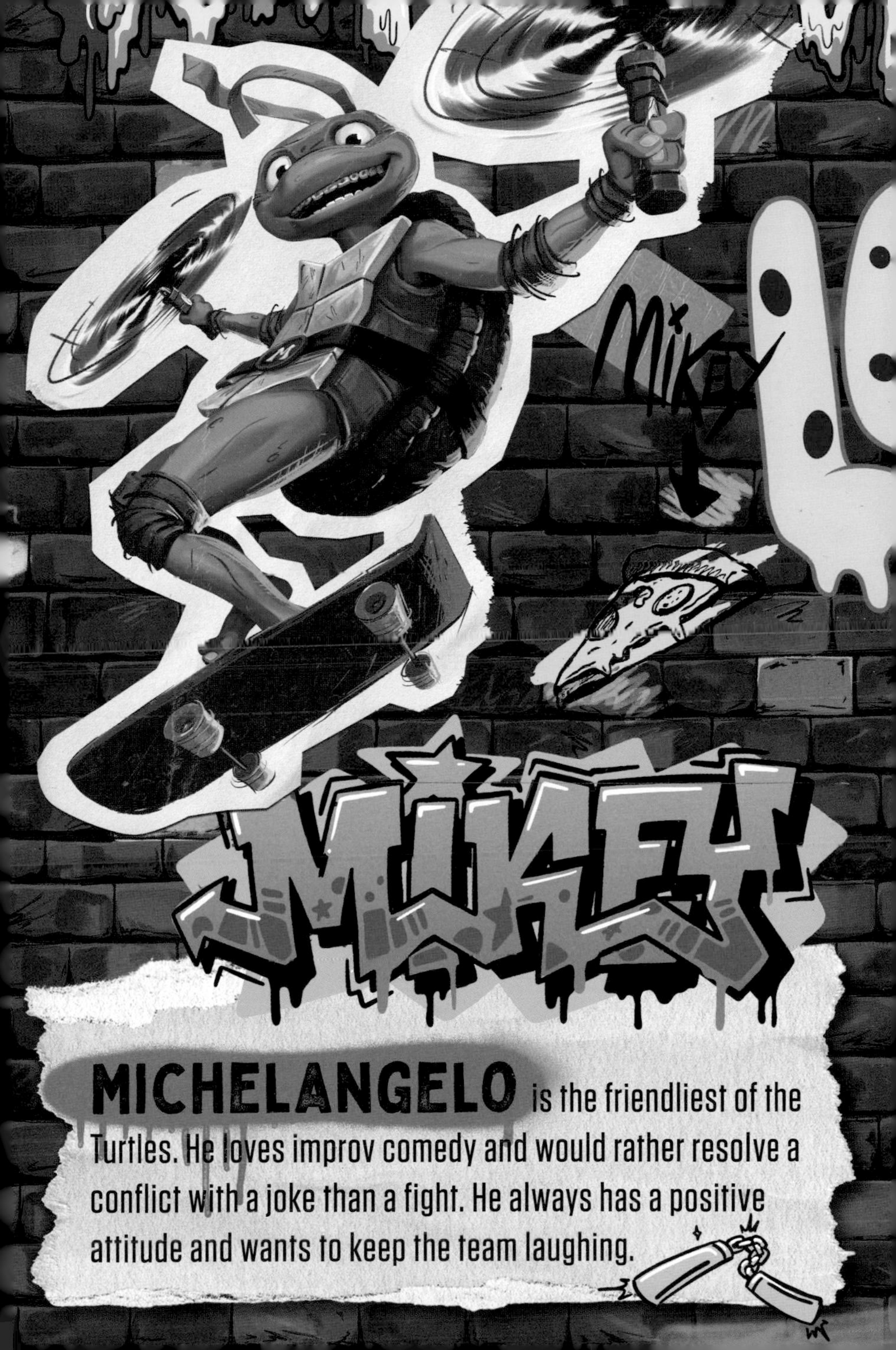

MICHELANGELO is the friendliest of the Turtles. He loves improv comedy and would rather resolve a conflict with a joke than a fight. He always has a positive attitude and wants to keep the team laughing.

DONATELLO is the brains behind his brothers' brawn. Donnie can sometimes seem a little arrogant, but that's just because he knows there's so much he has to offer the world!

SPLINTER is wise and patient. He is more than a teacher, he is also a father figure to the Turtles. He found them when they were young and taught them ninjutsu.

APRIL is a young journalist and the first human to befriend the Turtles. She's investigating criminal activity led by a mysterious figure named Superfly. She thinks the Turtles can help her put a stop to him.

BEBOP AND ROCKSTEADY

are NYC's Most Wanted! Not all mutants are good. Bebop and Rocksteady are two of the meanest dudes working for Superfly. They are pure mutant muscle . . . though they aren't very bright.

TURTLE POWER!
IT'S TURTLE TIME!
Leo, Raph, Mikey, and Donnie are ready for action. With teamwork, training, helpful friends, and some tasty pizza, they know they can keep New York City safe!

It was closed, but Superfly easily smashed the front door in, turning the CLOSED sign to OPEN as he sauntered through. He flipped a bunch of switches with his claw, and the bowling alley came to life. Lights snapped on. Games beeped and dinged. Music played. Smiling, the mutants settled in to have some fun and get to know each other.

Raph, Bebop, and Rocksteady walked up to a punching-bag game. Raph walloped the bag! *PA-WHAMP!* Bells rang, and the score at the very top of the column lit up. Bebop punched the bag even harder, ripping it right off the machine. *SHWACKKK!* With no bag left to punch, Rocksteady just picked up the whole contraption and slammed it into the wall, smashing it to pieces. *CRASH!*

The three mutants laughed together. "Man," Raph said, wiping his eyes, "you guys get it! I think you guys are my new best friends!"

By the jukebox, Donnie was checking out the musical selections with Wingnut and Leatherhead. "So," Donnie asked Wingnut, "what do you do when you're not working for Superfly?"

"Oh, me?" Wingnut asked. "I mostly play video

games. I read a lot. Comic books, anime . . ."

"I love anime!" Donnie said, grinning.

"Anime this, anime that, blah, blah, blah," Leatherhead said, tired of hearing Wingnut hold forth on the subject. "How about we talk about some footy?" she asked, referring to the sport of rugby football.

"Ugh," Wingnut grunted. "Ignore her, honestly. Do you know that all Australians are basically criminals?" Leaning into the jukebox for a better look, Leatherhead bumped into Wingnut. "Hey, watch the wings, mate!"

"Sorry, sorry," Leatherhead apologized.

Bowling with Mondo Gecko, Mikey was comparing favorite foods, beverages, bands, and TV shows. They kept getting perfect matches on their likes and dislikes. "Okay," Mikey said, picking up a bowling ball. "On three, we say our favorite movie. One, two, three . . ."

At the same time, Mikey and Mondo Gecko said, *"The Fault in Our Stars!"*

"Ahhhh!" Mondo Gecko cried out, amazed at yet another perfect match.

"I cry every time!" Mikey admitted.

"I just wish they could have been together!" Mondo Gecko said, referring to the two main characters in the tearjerker movie.

"Me too!" Mikey said.

Scumbug came up and started chittering away in Vermin. Mondo Gecko translated for her. "She says she only likes action movies with bugs in them."

From her nearby spot, April watched the outside of the bowling alley. She spoke into her earpiece. "Hey, guys? What's going on in there?"

Standing near Superfly, Leo quietly spoke into his own earpiece. "Still not sure, if I'm being honest."

"Well, ask him more questions!" April snapped impatiently. "Figure out what the heck is going on with this dude!"

Ray Fillet laid a bunch of snacks out on a big table. Gathering around, everyone started to eat, but Genghis Frog snatched up half the food with one stretch of his long tongue.

Holding a plate of food, Leo sidled up to Superfly. "So, uh, maybe you could finish explaining, like, exactly where you came from and what you want and stuff."

"What do I want?" Superfly said, smiling. "Easy. Acceptance."

The Turtles looked at each other.

"No way, man!" Leo gasped. "We want that, too!"

Donnie gestured toward his gang of mutants. "But look at your friends, man. Look at your crew. Don't you have that?"

"Let me go back to the start," Superfly said.

Superfly leaned back against a wall, remembering. "My earliest memory in the world is being loved by my dad. Him telling me that he never was accepted. Never was loved by anyone else. He just wanted a family, man. That's why he created us."

Leo listened closely, amazed that this fly man, so strong and fierce-looking, could speak so tenderly of his early days with his father. Donnie, Mikey, and Raph were caught up in Superfly's story, too. The eight other mutants had heard the story before but were always happy to hear Superfly tell it again.

"But then the people my dad worked for took it all away from him," Superfly said. "I rescued my little baby brothers and sisters, and since I was the oldest, I had to raise them. But we made the best of it. We found a place to live—a place where they throw away broken boats and ships by the water. There we'd do things together. Just normal things. You know, watch TV shows—"

"Like *Party of Five*!" Wingnut said enthusiastically, remembering a favorite show from that time. In the show, five siblings had to get by on their own after their parents died in a car accident. The oldest boy was in charge, kind of like Superfly.

"And he raised us *so* well," Bebop said, smiling at Superfly.

"He did," Rocksteady agreed. "I mean, look at us."

"I think we're very well-adjusted, too," Bebop said.

"A bunch of mates, eh?" Leatherhead said. "Real tight. Really tight."

It all sounded very familiar to the Turtles. Hiding from humans. Sneaking out to take what they needed. Only having each other. Depending on each other for everything. Being a family.

Superfly nodded. "But still, we deserved more,

right? We thought, 'These humans murdered our dad, but maybe they're not *all* bad,' you know?"

The Turtles nodded. They were certain that there were plenty of good humans, even if their father disagreed with them.

"So we went out and hit the town," Superfly said. "And, well . . . it didn't go well."

Leatherhead remembered that trip. "Crikey, the humans went bonkers!" The crew of mutants all nodded, remembering how the humans had reacted that day.

"They did not like it," Wingnut agreed, recalling their frightened faces. "Not big fans."

"Lot of hate," Leatherhead explained. "Lot of vitriol, really."

"This one dude especially," Superfly said. "He wouldn't stop chasing us. He wanted to *kill* us! So you know what I did?"

Donnie raised his hand. "You decided to go into hiding until you came up with a plan to make humans accept you as one of them?" That, after all, had pretty much been the Turtles' plan.

"Nah," Superfly snarled. "I beat that dude within

an inch of his life. Mollywhopped that fool! POW!" The beating Superfly had given the guy that day had been so severe that the other mutants had felt troubled as they'd watched it go down.

"And as I saw the fear in that human's eyes," Superfly continued, clearly relishing the memory, "I knew what to do—make humans scared to death of us, kill them all, and let MUTANTS RULE THE EARTH!"

"Ooookay," Mikey said slowly. "Sort of a twist . . ."

"Kind of a curveball," Raph said.

As she listened through her earpiece, April's eyes widened. "Okay, don't really love that. . . ."

Mondo Gecko could see that the Turtles weren't entirely comfortable with Superfly's plan. "We wish there was another way to feel safe and happy, but peoples . . . they gotta go."

The Turtles looked at each other uneasily.

"I inherited my dad's mind for science," Superfly continued. "And I thought, 'What if I build a machine to solve our problems?' Slowly, we came up with a plan to build it. And for the last few months, we've been *crushing* it, right?"

Wingnut considered this. “I mean, I feel pretty good about things.”

“It’s been pretty good!” Bebop agreed.

But Leatherhead was more enthusiastic. “Smashing it, mate!”

“Three thumbs up!” Wingnut said, deciding to be more positive.

Raph scratched his head. He was pretty sure they needed more details. “And so . . . about this machine that you were making . . .”

“What does it do, exactly?” Leo asked.

“It’s actually simple,” Superfly replied. “It’s gonna use a little of my blood to create a weaponized version of ooze. Thanks again for that word, by the way. So much better than *sludge.* Anyway, then the machine’s gonna launch the weaponized ooze into the atmosphere to vaporize! Here’s the kicker: every animal on Earth will be transformed into a mutant. Every fly, flea, tick, snake, fish, and whale. Everything. We mutants will become the dominant species on Earth!” He made a little concluding gesture with his claw, as if to say, “And that will be that!”

Into the Turtles' earpieces, April said, "That's bad. That's very bad."

But Donnie still held out hope. He wanted to be sure, so he asked, "What happens to humans in this plan of yours?"

Superfly turned, looking straight at Donnie.

"Nothing good!" Superfly said. "A bunch will be eaten. Others turned into a fuel of some sort. Maybe they become a form of entertainment, know what I mean? You know how they used to have the dog shows and the horse races? Well, maybe we'll have, like, tall guy shows and redhead races or something. You know, I'll think of something stupid."

"Wow, that's even worse," April said over the earpieces.

"They should be pets!" Rocksteady announced.

"I'm gonna throw 'em on a barbie!" Leatherhead promised, meaning a barbecue.

"You wanna throw *everything* on the barbie!"

Wingnut chided. "For goodness' sake!"

Superfly held up both claws. "Honestly, I'm open to all ideas if you've got any. Any crazy thing y'all think of, I want to do it. Just pitch 'em to me soon, because now that I've got the assimilator . . ." He led the way out of the bowling alley and over to the back of the van. "I can complete my device, and acceptance will be ours!" His gang of mutants cheered.

The Turtles looked at each other. What could they say? They certainly didn't like Superfly's plan for dealing with Earth's humans, including April. But they also were pretty sure he wouldn't react well to anyone trying to stop him from carrying it out.

"So what's up? You wanna roll with us?" Superfly asked. "'Cause we can activate the machine tonight!" He shook his head, laughing. "It's *crazy* that we met on the very night we're gonna take over the world. That's in the stars! It was meant to be!"

Urgently speaking into the Turtles' earpieces, April said, "So just checking in . . . you stopping them now? Or you gonna make me film you supplying an evil villain with the last piece of his horrible puzzle? You're gonna stop him? You're GONNA STOP HIM?! Somebody! Just talk so I know you're gonna stop him."

"Working on it," Leo said to April through his com device. He addressed Superfly directly. "Yo, uh, Superfly. So what if we're actually, like—I don't know, I'm just getting silly here—what if we're not into the plan? What if we don't like it? What would happen?"

"Yeah," Raph chimed in, stepping next to Leo. "Just hypothetically speaking, obviously."

All of the mutants, who had been moving toward the van to unload the assimilator, stopped in their tracks and turned to face the Turtles.

"Well," Superfly said slowly, "that would mean that I was wrong about you. And you're not as cool as I thought you were. And that right there . . . would make me mad." *WHAM!* He stomped on a fire hydrant, crushing it like an aluminum can.

"Whoa!" the Turtles called out, taking a step back.

Superfly took a threatening step toward the brothers. "I'm about to go to one hundred on y'all!"

"No, no, no!" the Turtles cried, holding up their hands. "We're cousins, remember?"

Superfly shook his head, looking disgusted. "Drop that cousin stuff right now. This has got nothing to do with cousins."

Leo smiled, trying to calm Superfly down. "Listen, man," he said. "We were just joking around, because we are in fact very *into* your plan."

Superfly narrowed his gaze, staring at the Turtles. "All right," he finally said. "Cool."

"Your plan's great," Leo said. "I love the killing-people part."

"I'll cut around that," April said into the Turtles' ears.

Donnie quietly told his brothers, "Guys, I've got an idea." Turning to Superfly and his crew, he said, "So, S-fly, we'll drive the van with the storage unit while you lead the way!"

"Yes!" Raph agreed. "Great thinking!"

"Just drop us a pin on our phones, and we'll meet you at your hideout with the device," Mikey said.

"Nice," April said, thinking this was how the Turtles were going to keep the assimilator out of Superfly's claws. "Smooth."

"Cool, but I drive fast," Superfly said. "Don't want

y'all to get lost." He turned to his crew. "Mondo, Wingnut, Rock—ride with the tortoises."

"Not so nice," April said. If Superfly's mutant crew were going to ride along with the Turtles, how were they supposed to dispose of the assimilator?

"I'll drive!" Mondo Gecko said.

"You're good to drive?" Raph said, watching the lizard's weird eyes roll in different directions.

Mondo Gecko laughed. "No!"

"Oh, hey!" Rocksteady shouted, excited. "I call shotgun! You know I get carsick in the backseat." He headed for the front passenger seat.

"I'll see you in, like, twenty minutes," Bebop told his friend.

"How long is that?" Rocksteady asked.

"We'll phone each other on the way," Bebop assured him.

"Ooh! Van ride with our new friends!" Wingnut cooed. "Yay!"

"Dang it," April said into her mic, frustrated that Superfly had foiled Donnie's plan.

The Turtles climbed into the back of the van with the

assimilator, trapped and terrified. Mondo Gecko peeled out, driving away from the Brooklyn Bridge. Superfly's two tricked-out custom cars and one motorcycle followed them.

In the front seat, the three mutant gangsters argued about what to play on the radio. "Spice Girls!" Wingnut called out, voting for a girl group popular in the '90s. "Put 'em on!"

"You don't like Phish?!" Mondo Gecko asked in disbelief. The band's hippie-style music was his absolute favorite.

"What? Phish? No! Spice Girls!" Wingnut insisted.

"Jam bands are the best, bro!" Mondo Gecko claimed.

"No," Wingnut said, shaking her head. "Jam is something you put on toast."

Mondo Gecko tried to think of an alternative to the Spice Girls. "You like Brandi Carlile?" he suggested, referring to a popular singer-songwriter who'd won a bunch of Grammys.

But Wingnut wasn't swayed. "British culture! The '90s! Come on—put it on!"

Donnie leaned forward from the back of the van.

"Hey, uh, where are we going, exactly?"

"Oh! See that building over there?" Mondo Gecko asked. "That's not it." He laughed at his own joke. "No, we're going to this super-cool shipping graveyard in Staten Island. It's the best New York borough, bro." Superfly's hideout was a derelict freighter in a ship graveyard just off Staten Island.

As they wound through the streets of Brooklyn, April followed on her scooter, struggling to keep up. "Okay, it's go time!" she said into her mic. "Attack these fools!"

Whispering into his own mic, Raph said, "Not sure that's as easy as it sounds. This dude is a literal rhinoceros man." Rocksteady looked like he could certainly hold his own in a fight. And who knew what Mondo Gecko and Wingnut were capable of?

"Enough of this song already," Mondo Gecko said, changing the station. Wingnut argued with him, paying no attention to the Turtles' quiet conversation.

Leo whispered, "If we jam the brakes, they'll just fly out the front of the car. Since Superfly ripped it off, there's no windshield to stop them."

Mikey looked doubtful. "It's impossible. We'd need, like, a long and narrow device that's small enough to get under the seat, but strong enough to press the brake pedal."

Donnie brightened up. "You mean . . . a stick?"

Mondo Gecko, Wingnut, and Rocksteady were happily singing along to the radio. It was blasting out a song by the band 4 Non Blondes.

"Love this song," Donnie said, hoping the mutants would be so caught up in their singing that they wouldn't notice what he was doing in the backseat.

The Turtles braced themselves. Donnie carefully snaked his bo staff under the driver's seat. Mondo Gecko's foot was pressing down on the gas pedal. But Donnie shoved his stick against the brake pedal, slamming it all the way to the floor. *SCREEEEE!* The van screeched to a stop. Mondo Gecko, Wingnut, and Rocksteady flew out of the van. As Mondo Gecko flew, he twisted his head around and looked at Mikey. "WHAT'S . . . GOING . . . ON?!" he cried.

"Sorrryyyyyyy!" Mikey called to him.

The three mutants tumbled onto the street. Donnie scrambled into the driver's seat, made a hard turn, and sped off, leaving Mondo Gecko, Wingnut, and Rocksteady lying in the road, wondering what had just happened.

From his car, Superfly saw his three siblings hit the ground and the van take off. "What are those Turtles doing?! GET THOSE FOOLS!"

The three cars raced after the van. Donnie floored it, swerving wildly through the streets of Brooklyn. With no windshield, the Turtles were buffeted by the rushing night air. "If I had hair, this would be a disaster!" Mikey cried.

The Turtles kept speeding through the streets, trying to shake their pursuers. Recording all the action from her scooter, April spoke to the Turtles through her mic. "You guys better hurry! Superfly's catching up!"

Bebop's oversized vehicle roared up alongside the Turtles' van. "Why'd you toss Rocksteady out of the van? He's very sensitive!" Donnie tried to ram Bebop's truck into the cars parked along the side of the road. "Whoa!"

Bebop yelled, driving right over the parked cars. "You can't stop me! It's a monster truck, dummies!"

Mondo Gecko leapt onto the roof. "Hey, dudes!" he said, leaning down to address the Turtles. "You launched me out the front of the van! Not cool!"

"I'm so sorry!" Mikey apologized. "We had to!"

"You know what?" Mondo Gecko asked. "I don't accept that apology!"

"Yeah, I'm not sorry at all; I'm not gonna lie!" Raph said, punching Mondo Gecko in the face and sending him flying off the van. He managed to land on his tail's roller skate and grab on to the van's bumper. He skated alongside the van, holding on tight.

Meanwhile, Rocksteady sideswiped the van with his motorcycle. "Why would you do that?" he asked. "I thought we were friends!" Donnie struggled to control the wheel.

Through the windows, Leatherhead snapped her huge jaws. "Come on, blokes!" she shouted. "Just give us the van! Give us the van!"

"No!" Leo shouted back. "We can't let you kill all the humans!"

Wingnut swooped in front of the van, flapping her mechanical wings. She looked back at Superfly, speeding after them in his muscle car. "Pull over!" she yelled. "Superfly is almost here, and he's not going to be as nice about this!"

"You're not being nice!" Leo pointed out.

"He'll be less nice!" Wingnut said.

"Hey, Wingnut, I thought we were cool!" Donnie said. "I thought we liked the same things!"

Still skating alongside the van, Mondo Gecko popped up into view. "We were cool! But we're too deep into this plan, bro! I don't know what to tell you."

"We've got nothing else, fellas!" Leatherhead explained. "This is our only path forward!"

"Superfly is our only family!" Wingnut added. "Is he perfect? No!"

Bebop called out from his monster truck, "Oh, he has problems. He has massive issues!"

"He's not Dad of the Year," Rocksteady admitted from his motorcycle, "but he's *our* dad."

This heartfelt conversation was interrupted by Superfly ramming the back of the van. *KA-WHAAAAAM!*

The van's back wheels were lifted off the ground!

"Now or never, dudes!" Mondo Gecko warned, giving the Turtles one last chance before they would face Superfly's wrath. "Give us the device!"

In his sleek, powerful racing car, Superfly had Genghis Frog take the wheel. Then he climbed out onto the hood and effortlessly ripped the back off the van. *SKREEE-AAAANK!*

Adjusting his rearview mirror, Donnie saw Superfly towering on the hood of the car behind them, huge and terrifying. "Can someone please try stopping the supervillain?" Donnie begged.

"Aw, okay," Raph sighed. Using his most intimidating voice, he faced off with Superfly and said, "Let's go."

The hulking mutant knocked Raph out with a single punch of his claw.

Leo tried to draw one of his swords, but in the cramped quarters of the van, already filled with the assimilator, it wasn't easy to swing the weapon. He ended up getting it stuck in the roof. Superfly grabbed Leo's other sword and pinned him against the wall with it.

Mikey whipped his nunchucks. *SNIP!* Superfly cut the

chains with his claws, rendering the weapon useless.

"Guys, status update?" Donnie called back over his shoulder as he drove.

"Not good!" Mikey said, holding up his worthless nunchucks. Superfly had put all three Turtles out of commission in a matter of seconds.

Superfly grabbed the assimilator, lifted it out of the van, and loaded it onto his car. Reaching through to the van's dashboard, he ripped the steering wheel off its column! Then he grabbed Donnie's bo staff and pushed it against Donnie's foot, pressing it down on the gas pedal. Wedging the other end of the staff against the roof of the van, Superfly forced the Turtles to zoom through the night with no way to steer!

"Oh no!" Donnie cried. "He used the stick against me!"

"Man, I almost thought y'all was cool," Superfly said with regret. "Goodbye forever, cousin Turtles!"

Superfly jumped back into his car and peeled off with the assimilator.

KUUU-WHACK! The van crashed off a freeway overpass with the Turtles screaming inside!

THWAMP! The van landed nose-down on the street, wrecked beyond repair. T.C.R.I. vehicles full of soldiers pulled up, surrounding the crash site.

"Go, go, go, go!" the commander barked. "Surround them! Make a perimeter!"

As the Turtles stumbled out of the wreckage, the soldiers stared at them, amazed to see bizarre mutants instead of Bad Bernie's gang. They raised their weapons, aiming right at the four brothers.

Leo spotted April on her scooter. "April," he said into his mic. "Help." But then he watched, astonished, as she turned and drove away, speeding off into the night. The Turtles couldn't believe she'd abandoned them.

At T.C.R.I. headquarters, Utrom was able to watch her team's progress on a monitor, thanks to the soldiers' helmet cameras. A soldier reported, "Ms. Utrom, we've lost the signal on the assimilator, but we've recovered these . . . things." He gestured toward the Turtles.

"Yes," Utrom said triumphantly. Stockman's mutants! After all these years! "Bring them to me!"

"Yes, ma'am," the soldier said. He turned to the Turtles. "Say good night, freaks."

Soldiers knocked the Turtles out, threw them into their vehicles, and caravanned to T.C.R.I. headquarters, where Cynthia Utrom was waiting for her prize. She knew exactly what she would do with the mutants. . . .

When the brothers came to, they found themselves in a glass cage, strapped to tables and hooked up to diabolical machines. "What's happening?" Leo asked. "Hey! Let us out! Come on!"

On the other side of the glass, a heavily armed security team guarded the cage. Cynthia Utrom stepped forward, gloating. "Why, hello, Turtles. I've been looking for you for a long, long time."

Strapped to a table, Donnie craned his neck as best

he could to meet Utrom's fierce gaze. "Look, lady!" he said angrily. "I don't know what you want from us, or why you talk so scary, but we shouldn't be here! There's a fly monster—"

ZZAP! Utrom pressed a button, shocking Donnie with a jolt of electricity. "I will do the talking," she said calmly. "I am Cynthia Utrom, and you are my property."

Leo looked baffled. "What do you mean, your prop—"

ZZAP! Utrom shocked the Turtles.

"Hey!" Raph protested.

ZZAP! Another shock.

"Stop!" Mikey cried.

ZZAP!

"Enough!" Utrom ordered. "I will use you to complete our glorious work. Your blood will allow me to create a stable mutagen. And with that mutagen, I will create an army of super soldiers!" She held up a blueprint of a human with the fins and flippers of a dolphin. "Dolphin men to plant bombs on submarines." She held up another blueprint, this one of a human with long wings and a sharp beak. "Eagle men to fight enemy jets." A third blueprint showed a human with the head and body of a snake. "Snake men to slither behind enemy lines."

She set the blueprints down, looking moved by her own vision. "The glory of it all nearly brings me to tears." Utrom turned toward the Turtles with a terrifyingly fierce expression on her face. "My army of super mutants will live! I will milk you dry! I WILL MILK YOU DRY!"

"AHHH!" the brothers screamed. "Dad was right!"

Utrom turned to her scientists. "START THE MILKING MACHINE!"

Superfly soon reached his hideout with the assimilator and loaded it into his lab. Now all he had to do was connect the assimilator to his massive doomsday machine, built according to Baxter Stockman's plans. He punched a button, and the huge machine rumbled to life. *VRUM-VRUM-VRUM-VRUM . . .*

In the Turtles' sewer home, Splinter sat alone, sadly watching the balloons he'd put out for the pizza party deflate. Sighing, he flipped through a family photo album. In the early pictures, when the boys were young Turtles, they looked happy posing with their dad. In the middle shots, as they grew older, they started to look more distant. And in the most recent photos, the teenaged Turtles looked miserable, unhappy to pose for yet another picture in the sewers, where they felt trapped.

Hearing footsteps behind him, Splinter sprang to his feet, full of hope. "Boys?!" he cried. "You came home? You forgive me? My surprise party worked?"

He turned to see not his beloved sons, but a human!

"AHH!" he screamed.

Holding up both hands to show she meant him no harm, April said, "Heyyyyy, Mr. Rat . . . Man. You might want to sit down."

In Cynthia Utrom's secret lab at T.C.R.I. headquarters, Splinter's worse prediction about what would happen if humans got ahold of the Turtles was coming true.

Mikey was getting milked!

"AAAHHH!" he screamed. "Stop it!"

Leo grimaced. "That looks bad."

"Does it hurt?" Donnie asked.

"Of course it hurts!" Mikey cried. "She's milking me!" Restrained and attached to tubes, Mikey was having his ooze-blood milked into a large container. His brothers' turns attached to the ooze-milking machine were coming.

"Try to think of something pleasant!" Raph suggested. "To take your mind off the pain!"

"Yeah, think of pizza!" Leo said, knowing pizza was Mikey's favorite. "Think of the pizza!"

Mikey tried, closing his eyes. Then he popped them open. "Pizza's made of cheese! And cheese is made of MILK! And I'm being milked! It's infiltrated my every thought! *AAHHHH!*"

"I'm so sorry, Mikey!" Leo said sympathetically.

"All right," Cynthia Utrom said, having heard enough. She gestured toward the large container. "We'll milk you until we have the required amount. See you not so soon, Turtles." She turned and left the laboratory.

Assistants attached Raph to the milking apparatus. "This is it, guys," he said. "We're gonna die here. Getting milked to death in a lab!"

"I always knew it would end like this," Mikey claimed.

His brothers didn't buy it. "Shut up, Mikey," Donnie said.

"No, you didn't," Raph said.

"Such a liar," Leo said.

Even though they were roughly teasing Mikey in their usual way, all of them were well aware of the serious trouble they were in. Things did not look good. At all.

"I can't believe April just left us," Leo said. "Maybe she was just using us all along."

"Well, she ended up getting a great story," Raph said, not minding being distracted from the ooze-extraction process. "I can see the headline: 'TURTLE BOYS GIVE SUPERVILLAIN LAST PART OF HIS EVIL MACHINE.'"

"You know," Leo said. "That's actually a pretty good title."

"Yeah, very clickbait-y," Donnie agreed.

"I'd definitely give that a read," Mikey said.

Donnie sighed. "I guess we were stupid to think humans would ever like us."

"We're naive!" Raph said.

"We're so naive we destroyed the planet!" Mikey cried. "That's why we're unlikable!"

"I wish I got to travel more, you know?" Leo shared.

"I wish I had a girlfriend," Raph admitted.

"I wish I could have tried frozen yogurt!" Mikey cried with anguish.

Leo looked puzzled. "You could have."

"I know!" Mikey yelped. "And I blew it!"

Leo shook his head sadly. "It would have been nice to go out with a show."

Donnie nodded. "It would have been nice."

Suddenly all the lights in the room went out!

Outside the cell holding the Turtles, the T.C.R.I. guards went on high alert the second the lights went out.

"Someone's here!" one of them shouted. "Stay alert!"

In her office, Cynthia Utrom heard an alarm go off. Guards rushed into the room. "What's happening?" she demanded.

"There's an intruder," the lead guard explained. "We have to get you to a secure location."

"But did the milking stop?!" she asked. Without answering, the guards quickly escorted her to a safe room with a blast-proof metal door.

Back in the darkened laboratory with the ooze-milking equipment, guards searched for the unseen intruder with their weapons drawn. Then, from a vent in the ceiling, Splinter dropped to the floor. "Boys!" he cried.

"DAD!" the Turtles shouted in joy and astonishment.

The guards started to move toward the mutant rat man. "Stay back!" he warned. "I just came for my boys, who lied to me! They are in so much trouble right now!"

The brothers didn't like the sound of that. "We're actually good," Leo said.

"We can stay a little longer," Donnie added.

"It's fine," Mikey claimed.

The head guard wasn't fazed by Splinter's warning. "Yeah, right, freak," he scoffed. Turning to the other guards, he ordered, "Grab another machine and hook him up like the others."

"No!" Raph shouted. "Come on! Leave him alone!"

"He's old!" Leo pointed out. "He hasn't been in a fight in . . . I don't know if he's *ever* been in a fight."

The Turtles were glad their father had come to rescue them, but what could the old rat possibly do against a team of heavily armed T.C.R.I. soldiers?

Plenty, it turned out.

Putting on an unbelievable display of ninja moves, Splinter spun, whirled, kicked, and punched his way around the room, never stopping, swiftly taking all the soldiers down, sometimes singly, and sometimes more than one at a time. It was incredible!

"WHOA!" the brothers yelled, amazed.

"Yeah!" Mikey cried. "Kick his butt, Dad!"

"Yeah, get him, Dad!" Leo cheered.

"Yeah, go, Dad!" Donnie and Raph called at the same time.

A guard spoke into his walkie-talkie. "Requesting backup!"

Reinforcements poured into the lab, and Splinter found himself in the fight of his life. Seriously outnumbered, he had to call on all his martial arts skills *and* his abilities as a rat, squeezing himself through tiny openings, gnawing with his long teeth, and whipping his tail to knock tubes and beakers at his assailants. More than once it looked as though he had been defeated, but he always rallied, fiercely fighting his way back until eventually he won the battle. The soldiers were down.

Smacking a button on a control panel, Splinter released his sons from their cage.

"DAD!" they all cried once again, rushing to embrace him.

"Boys!" Splinter said, hugging them back. "Are you okay?"

They assured him they were fine. "How did you find us?" Leo asked.

April dropped into the room through a vent. "I mean, I'd be a pretty big jerk if I didn't at least try to get your dad to come help you."

"April!" Leo shouted, thrilled to see her. He'd absolutely hated the idea that she would abandon the Turtles in their hour of need.

Splinter walked over to April's side. "Yes, this *human* you are apparently friends with told me you lied to me! What happened? What have you been doing?"

"N-nothing," the Turtles stammered, not ready to share their plan for fame, glory, and human adulation.

Splinter noticed the apparatus Cynthia Utrom had been using to extract the Turtles' mutant ooze. "Wait a minute," he said. "What is this machine?"

The brothers all answered at once.

"Uh, this machine?"

"It's nothing!"

"I think it's an extraction machine."

Splinter peered at a metal tag on the mechanism. "Does that say *milking machine*?"

The Turtles tried to deny that their father had been right all along.

"No!"

"It's the opposite of that!"

April looked at the tag. "It's a milking machine."

Splinter gestured toward the milking machine. "See! I told you they'd milk you! This is why I told you not to leave the sewer! Why would you lie to me?!"

Leo put up his hands to calm their dad down. "Okay, look," he said, coming clean. "We thought if we could stop this really bad criminal named Superfly that maybe—*maybe*—we could be liked by humans. And I guess we just didn't think you'd understand."

Splinter stood motionless, listening. Then he burst out with, "You are right, I don't understand! Now come, let's go home before these men wake up."

One of the guards stirred. Splinter knocked him out again with a clean sweep of his foot. "See? Like this guy!"

Once they were outside the T.C.R.I. building, April went one way, while Splinter and the Turtles went another. They were headed for Staten Island.

When the Turtles and Splinter arrived at the boat graveyard, Superfly's hideout was easy to spot. Only one boat had lights shining through its windows—a crumbling, abandoned freighter.

The brothers and their father made their way down into Superfly's laboratory below the deck, ready for action. They found the huge machine designed to cover the world with ooze, but no mutants. "Maybe they decided to just, like, give up and go bowling?" Mikey suggested.

Superfly's voice emerged from the shadows. "Naaaah, fam . . ."

He and his crew stepped into the light. "We're just

one step ahead of y'all!" Superfly said.

Splinter struck a martial arts pose. "I don't want to fight a fellow mutant, but I will!"

Superfly shook his monstrous head. "Y'all just won't quit, huh? What is it about these stinkin' humans that you love so much?"

"It's not just us!" Leo pointed out. "You like human stuff, too!"

Mondo Gecko made a confused, disgusted face. "No, we don't!"

"Yes, you do!" Mikey insisted. "Take the band Phish. Contrary to their name, they're comprised entirely of—"

"Fish!" Mondo Gecko interrupted.

"No!" Mikey said.

"Humans?!" Mondo Gecko guessed, amazed.

"Yes!" Mikey confirmed.

Donnie raised his hands and smiled. "See? Humans are complicated creatures! They're good, like April. And they're bad, like that lady who milked us."

Superfly's mutants looked confused. Milked them?

Splinter joined his sons' plea. "And as much as I don't like them—and trust me, I do NOT like them—if we murder them, we're no better than they are."

Leo could see that the gang members were listening. He pressed the point. "I refuse to accept that you all are cool with brutally killing all the humans! You just can't be! You're awesome! You're fun. We . . . vibed."

Much as he liked vibing, Mondo Gecko still wasn't sure about the Turtles' argument. "But killing off the humans is the only way we'll ever be accepted!"

Raph shook his head. "That's not true."

"We accept you!" Mikey said sincerely.

Leo got an idea. "Come live with us!"

Splinter was immediately on board with this suggestion. He much preferred living in the sewers with fellow mutants to fighting them. Or dealing with humans up on the surface. "Yes!" he said. "Plenty of room!"

Superfly's mutant crew looked at each other. "I mean . . . ," Bebop said slowly.

"If I'm being honest . . . ," Rocksteady said, continuing his friend's sentence.

"I'd rather not murder tons of people," Wingnut said, finishing their thought. "I'm afraid I'll be haunted by the faces of my victims in my sleep!"

Mondo Gecko was touched by the invitation offered by the Turtles and their dad. "You'll really let us live with you?"

"Of course, bro!" Mickey said enthusiastically.

"Brah!" Mondo Gecko said, reaching toward him.

"Brah!" Mikey answered, stretching out his arms.

"Abracada-brah!" Mondo Gecko said as they hugged.

Superfly couldn't believe what he was hearing and seeing. "What're y'all doing?! Stop this kumbaya stuff and start killing these fools!"

Mondo Gecko broke away from Mikey to confront his boss. "No, we don't wanna do this! And really, I don't think we ever did! We just didn't think there was any alternative. But now that we've met these dudes, we see there is! Let's just stop and vibe!"

"Nah, man, I don't vibe," Superfly said. "I know y'all might think there's another way to be safe and happy, but you don't know what you're talking about. If you want that, you just gotta do what I say!"

Splinter looked pained. "Oh no," he groaned. "That's what I said." In trying to protect his sons from humans, had he been no different than Superfly?

"Seriously, Supe . . . ," Bebop said.

"Turn off the machine," Rocksteady told him, gesturing toward the huge apparatus.

Superfly cocked his head, a sneer forming on his lips, such as they were. "Or else what?"

His mutants froze, hesitating to attack their leader.

"Yeah, that's what I thought," Superfly said. He looked at the gigantic ooze vaporizer. "You wanna stop this machine, you gotta go through me!"

The mutants looked at each other. It was clear what they were thinking: *Are we really going to go through with this? Are we going to attack Superfly? The mutant who raised us?*

"Let's go, brah," Mondo Gecko said.

They charged Superfly!

"You can't beat me!" he shouted. "I know y'all! I know what you're gonna do before you do it!"

Not wanting to hurt their sibling, the mutants instead tried to destroy the machine. But every time one of them rushed at the apparatus, Superfly fended them off, tossing them aside like paper dolls.

Finally, by rushing Superfly together at the same

time, the mutants managed to shove him into the machine. *WHAMK!* The device started to shoot out sparks. When he saw that his creation might be damaged, Superfly started fighting even more fiercely. *"RAAHHHH!"* he roared in his fury.

The machine, shaking and sparking, powered up. Superfly tried to fight his way to its red launch button, but all the mutants managed to push him back. "Just STOP!" Leatherhead yelled.

"Please!" Mondo Gecko begged. "This isn't gonna make you happy!"

"NEVER!" Superfly bellowed. "Humans are evil! They have to pay!"

Summoning every ounce of his mutant strength to push past his siblings and cousins, he smacked the launch button with his claw! The mutants tackled him into the machine, sending bolts of power zapping through his body! Superfly was stuck to the device like a magnet on a refrigerator.

Rocksteady and Bebop charged the machine, slamming it through the wall of the rusty old boat. *CRAAAAASHHH!* Everyone watched through the gaping hole in the hull as the massive contraption and Superfly fell into the ocean with a tremendous splash. *SPLOOOOOOSH!*

The villain and his creation sank into the dark, cold water and disappeared. A few bubbles rose to the surface, then all was still in the moonlight.

"Did we stop it?" Mikey asked.

"I think so," Splinter said.

"And Superfly?" Donnie asked, peering into the black sea. "Is he . . . gone?"

The other mutants looked at each other. "I wouldn't count on it," Mondo Gecko said.

"Superfly's very tough," Bebop muttered.

"Super tough," Rocksteady agreed.

Everyone stared at the waves. For the moment, they had stopped Superfly from destroying human life on Earth. Most importantly, they'd done it together.

And if he ever came back, they knew they'd stop him again, no matter what his new plan might be. Working together as a family, the mutants felt as though they could tackle pretty much anything Superfly—or anyone else, for that matter—threw at them.

Mikey looked at his brothers, his father, and all the other mutants standing together. They looked strong and confident. They looked ready. Mikey drew a deep breath, and his chest swelled with pride. "Cowabunga," he murmured quietly.

TIME!
12:40 science!
NO RATS ALLOWED!
RAPH
NYC SEWER
HOME
WEAPON ROOM
TOILET
OUT
KITCHEN
TECH ROOM
THE STEELY BOYS
TURTLE POWER!
RAPH
UH OH
GO RHINOS
APRIL
SWORD 2
TO SEWER
GOING IN